VIKING

OLAF THE VIKING

MARTIN CONWAY

OXFORD
UNIVERSITY PRESS

OXFORD
UNIVERSITY PRESS

Great Clarendon Street, Oxford OX2 6DP

Oxford University Press is a department of the University of Oxford.
It furthers the University's objective of excellence in research, scholarship,
and education by publishing worldwide in

Oxford   New York

Auckland   Cape Town   Dar es Salaam   Hong Kong   Karachi
Kuala Lumpur   Madrid   Melbourne   Mexico City   Nairobi
New Delhi   Shanghai   Taipei   Toronto

With offices in

Argentina   Austria   Brazil   Chile   Czech Republic   France   Greece
Guatemala   Hungary   Italy   Japan   Poland   Portugal   Singapore
South Korea   Switzerland   Thailand   Turkey   Ukraine   Vietnam

Oxford is a registered trade mark of Oxford University Press
in the UK and in certain other countries

British Library Cataloguing in Publication Data

Data available

ISBN: 978-0-19-272087-0

1 3 5 7 9 10 8 6 4 2

Printed in Great Britain by CPI Cox and Wyman, Reading, RG1 8EX.

Paper used in the production of this book is a natural,
recyclable product made from wood grown in sustainable forests.
The manufacturing process conforms to the environmental
regulations of the country of origin.

For my amazing wife, Karen—the
harshest and most useful of critics,
and for my fantastic children,
Duncan, Thomas, and Natalie

CHAPTER ONE

Olaf looked at the pig.

The pig looked at Olaf.

Olaf reached for the rope on his belt, but then lost his balance, and slid a little down the slope. The pig barely looked up. Olaf retrieved his rope and tried another throw. This time, the loop dropped loosely on the pig's head, and Olaf managed to pull it tightly around the thick, grey neck. The pig began bucking and wriggling. Olaf released his hold on the sapling he'd been hanging on to, and gripped the rope with both hands. Suddenly he found himself tumbling downhill in the company of an indignant pig. There was a musical twang as the rope pulled tight. Another tree had stopped pig and boy just as they tumbled over a drop. At one end of the rope was the pig, swaying quietly; in the middle was the tree, which had brought a temporary halt to their tumble. At the other end was Olaf.

Olaf looked at the pig.

The pig looked at Olaf.

The pig wriggled his head sideways, and began to chew at the rope that was holding him over the drop.

Olaf had opened the hurdle-gate of the pen earlier that day with the intention of killing the pig. But he hadn't been able to bring himself to do it straight away. The pig had looked at him so piteously, as if he knew exactly what was going to happen, and as Olaf hesitated, knife in hand, the pig had lunged past him and then galloped off with Olaf running behind. The chase had lasted for hours, taking Olaf through marsh and mire, ravine and river, and, finally, up the steep-sided mountain from which he now found himself helplessly dangling.

For a moment, Olaf hung motionless, waiting for the drop. Then the pig paused to look at him before going back to work on the rope. Olaf wasn't very strong, it was true. On the other hand, Olaf wasn't very heavy, and he managed to swing himself, hand over hand, to within grasping distance of the ledge. He grabbed a tree-root and swung himself up, then scrambled to his feet, still gripping the rope. He summoned all his strength and tugged until the pig was dangling just under the ledge, then grabbed at the rope-ring round its neck and wrestled it up to safety.

Olaf straightened his clothes, and began the long walk home. The pig now trotted obediently, as though tumbling down a mountainside and dangling on a rope was a little hobby he indulged in most Sunday afternoons before dinner. As they went, Olaf rubbed some of the pig-dung from his face and eyes, and tidied his hair with the bone comb that had been his father's. By the time he was in sight of the village enclosure, most of the dung was gone, and he felt ready to present himself at the special meal that was to take place that night.

Kveld-Ulf was standing with his back to the fire, drinking deeply from a horn cup, surrounded by other men of the village. When he caught sight of the bedraggled Olaf, he bellowed with laughter.

'Well, look at that,' he choked. 'A piece of rope with a filthy animal at one end . . . and a pig at the other!'

Even the slave Loki, tied to a post nearby, joined in the fun.

'Nice to see you back again,' he shouted. Then he knelt and spoke confidentially in the pig's ear. 'But did you have to bring *him* with you?'

'Very funny,' Olaf snorted, tugging at the pig's tether.

Around the fire, the feast was already beginning, and the smell of roasting meat reminded him that he was achingly hungry. Grimnir had decided that it would be fun for the pig to join in, and took the tether to lead the animal towards the fire. Soon, the pig was happily settled on the ground, eating discarded crusts, and lapping from cups of mead which were offered from all directions.

As he took his place by the fire, Olaf could see that Uncle Kveld-Ulf was already well on the way to being drunk. But the meat tasted good, and there was plenty of it, in spite of the fact that one of the dishes that should have been on the menu was happily snorting and scrabbling for scraps. Olaf was exhausted, and sleep would soon have kidnapped him, if he hadn't been anxious to remind Kveld-Ulf about something close to his heart.

'Uncle Kveld-Ulf, you were going to make a speech.'

'So I was,' roared Kveld-Ulf. 'Quiet, you rabble.'

The enclosure lapsed into nervous silence.

'My people,' he bellowed, 'our ship is loaded and ready, and tomorrow we set off to scour the coasts of Normandy and Ireland and Angle-land and Scotland . . . '

'To look for my father!' Olaf interrupted.

'To look,' Kveld-Ulf continued, 'for gold.'

'And my father!' Olaf interrupted, anxiously.

'But of course,' Kveld-Ulf said, with a look at Olaf, 'I don't want anyone to think that gold and money is all that we care about.'

'Hooray!' shouted Olaf, and the pig grunted loudly, and nosed at a big puddle of spilt mead under the table.

'No, we also care about emeralds, and rubies, and diamonds.'

There was a great cheer, and Olaf tried desperately to raise his voice above it.

'What about my father?'

'Then, of course,' said Kveld-Ulf, 'there is the question of my dear brother—Olaf's father, Sigurd Toludsen. Has he been shipwrecked? Nobody knows. Where is he? Nobody knows. Is he alive or dead? Nobody cares! So here's to our treasure and plunder, and to Hel with Sigurd Toludsen!'

And with that, he downed another horn of mead, to the accompaniment of hilarious cheers from his followers.

Olaf said nothing at first. He thought of the weeks he had spent gutting and pickling herrings for the voyage, salting pork in barrels, grinding the meal for biscuits, heaving helmets and swords to the smith to be mended; and he thought of his father, who had left six long years ago, but whom he still remembered tossing him lightly into the air, and laughing, in the days when his mother had still been alive. In a kind of dream, Olaf went to fetch the steaming cauldron of sweet oats that had been simmering all day over a cooking fire. He walked around the table, to where Kveld-Ulf was still laughing at his joke. Kveld-Ulf impatiently gestured him to put the cauldron on the table, and he considered pouring the boiling mixture straight over his stupid hairy head. Then he caught sight of the pig, who by now was lying trotters upwards in a blissful drunken stupor, and paused for a moment before setting down the sweet oats in front of Kveld-Ulf.

'I'll get rid of the animal,' said Olaf, and he dragged the unconscious pig away.

If anyone had been watching, they might have noticed that Olaf took the pig, not in the direction of the pig-pen, but towards the longhouse in the middle of the enclosure. He returned soon enough, and then quietly ate, watching with disgust as Kveld-Ulf gobbled and guzzled and glugged. Finally, Kveld-Ulf stood, belched loudly, and staggered off through the darkness to collapse into his bed. It was so quiet when Kveld-Ulf was absent, that everyone decided that the best thing to do was to go to bed themselves. Olaf stayed by the dying fire as the last tired Viking stumbled off to bed, alone except for the slave Loki.

'I know it's a lot to ask,' said Loki, 'but I don't suppose I could be allowed to get within a mile or two of the fire? And a little food wouldn't kill me.'

Olaf took a small knife from his belt and sawed away at the cord holding Loki to his post. Loki rubbed at his wrists and eased himself towards the fire with difficulty. The iron manacles on his legs made it hard for him to move far or fast.

'Tell me about Angle-land, Loki.'

Loki took a piece of pork-fat from the table and chewed.

'You know the rhyme,' he said, 'what more is there to say?

'"Ireland's men are bald and holy,
Russia's men are lofty.
Vinland's men wear feathered crowns,
But Angles all are softies."'

'My father was planning to go to Angle-land,' Olaf said, thoughtfully.

'Then I imagine he's still alive,' said Loki. 'I gather he was a good fighter.'

'The best. He could . . . ' and Olaf tailed off, realizing that although he had been told by others that his father had been a fierce warrior, from what he remembered, he was gentle, and fun to be around.

'And if he went to Ireland?' asked Olaf.

'Oh, I think he'd survive there too. Vinland, of course, is another thing altogether. It's a long voyage, you see, to where the vines grow on the shores of the sea. And the people there, the Skraelings, as they're called, well . . . but why don't you find out for yourself?'

'What, me, go on a voyage? Why would I do that?'

'I thought you wanted to be reunited with your father.'

'I don't know,' said Olaf, 'I'm only twelve and . . . '

'I know, a trip like that would be too frightening for a little chap like you,' Loki twinkled.

'It's not that!' Olaf protested. 'It's just . . . well, I don't know the way to Angle-land.'

'Exactly. You'd need someone with you—someone more mature than yourself. Perhaps a slave, who would jump at a chance to escape . . . '

8

'Do you know anyone like that?' asked Olaf.

'Hmm. Now let me think . . . ' Loki rubbed his chin with his hand, as though deep in thought. 'That's a tough one. Someone who's being tied up as a slave, and would like to escape.'

'Just a minute,' Olaf said, brightly. '*You're* a slave, and you've been to Angle-land.'

'You're right!' Loki cried, as if the thought had just occurred to him. 'Only problem is . . . '

And he pointed at the shackles which fastened his legs together.

Why Olaf suddenly came to that drastic decision, he would never be able to explain to anyone, least of all himself. Perhaps he suddenly realized that with his mother dead and his father missing, there was no earthly reason why he had to stay, and almost any fate would be better than being bullied by Kveld-Ulf for the rest of his life. Olaf got up and trudged as quietly as his boots could carry him towards the longhouse.

All the tools and weapons were hung on a wall at the far end, where Kveld-Ulf slept. Olaf knew that what he needed was a large axe, but simply getting from one end of the longhouse to the other was going to be a problem in the dark. The heavy boards creaked as Olaf crept among the sleeping bodies. Carefully, he lifted the axe from its hooks, and began to stagger along under its weight. It wasn't long before disaster struck. His foot caught in a blanket wrapped around one of the sleepers, and he stumbled. As he tripped forwards, he felt the axe making contact with something soft. The only thing as soft as that, Olaf thought, was Grimnir's head. He was right! Grimnir began groaning, and scrambling to his feet. Olaf thought quickly. If Grimnir continued complaining, then Kveld-Ulf and all the others would soon be awake, and there would be no escape. He kicked at the spot where he guessed Grimnir's wife would be, and was rewarded with an agonized groan.

'Who's that?'

'It's me, my love. Grimnir.'

'Well, what you kicking me for?'

'Someone hit me.'

'Well, someone's going to hit you a lot harder if you don't get back to bed and stop kicking me.'

'I didn't.'

'Well, someone did, and you're the only one up.'

Another voice joined in.

'Will you two shut up!'

'Don't you tell me to shut up!'

As the squabbling continued, Olaf made his way to the door, and he was soon outside.

Loki was sitting by the fire, with his manacle propped on a stone, ready for Olaf to swipe it with the axe. The first blow did nothing. The second grazed Loki's thigh and made him howl quietly. The third bent the metal a little, but the fourth knocked off the head of the rivet that held the manacle together. One more swipe, and it opened enough for Loki to squeeze his leg out.

Things would probably have been different if Kveld-Ulf had stayed asleep. But it's a well-known fact that you are unlikely to enjoy a long and refreshing sleep when you are sharing your bed with a medium-sized pig. Kveld-Ulf had been slugged into unconsciousness by a gallon and a half of strong drink, and he awoke again just as suddenly, screaming with horror, convinced that he was being attacked by an evil spirit with big horny hooves and a wet nose. Kveld-Ulf squealed, the pig squealed, then Kveld-Ulf squealed even more. When the pig calmly trotted off in the direction of the fire, looking for more food and wine, Kveld-Ulf caught sight of his floppy ears silhouetted against the dying embers, and finally worked out what had happened.

A mean half-moon was swimming through thin clouds, but it was still too dark for Olaf to see Kveld-Ulf poking his head out of the door, or to watch his face contort with rage as he wiped the fresh pig-dung from his tunic, or to see him disappearing inside to find the biggest, nastiest weapon the village possessed in order to get his revenge. But Olaf could certainly *hear* Kveld-Ulf, whose bellowing was loud enough to start avalanches two countries away.

Olaf ran. Then he realized Loki still had a manacle on one leg, and came back to help him to his feet, and ran again—this time at the pace of a tortoise with a wooden leg. Kveld-Ulf and the others had gone back for more weapons, and after some painful clashes in the thin moonlight, gave chase at speed. Olaf began by heading for the boats, but then Loki took charge and changed direction, heading for the cliff path. He scrambled up the rocks with surprising agility, considering the rusty manacle that still hung from one leg. Olaf could hear Kveld-Ulf's clumsy bootsteps behind him as they stumbled along. He knew the place well. Three more paces and they would reach the edge of the cliff. That was when Loki began scrabbling desperately among the rocks, and then digging at the dirt with his nails. After a short while he had scooped a small hole in which there was the gleam of metal. Olaf watched, fascinated, as Loki began to tug the shining object from the hole. But soon he had to look away, because something more urgent was claiming his attention.

Kveld-Ulf was by a considerable margin the ugliest of the Vikings. He was also the fastest and angriest, and had been the first to scramble up the rocks. He had managed to find the most enormous sword the village possessed. Melted down, it would have yielded enough metal to arm an entire raiding-party and still have some left over for some fancy cloak-pins.

There was a moment when everything seemed to stop, giving Olaf the opportunity of a really good look up Kveld-Ulf's nostrils. Olaf could hear Kveld-Ulf's furious breathing as he brought the sword downwards. But the blow never reached its target. Sparks flew, there was a loud metallic clank, and then silence. For a moment, Kveld-Ulf stood dumb-struck, looking down at the gleaming metal object that had blocked the blow. Then he looked at Loki, who was still holding the thing, protecting Olaf from any further harm. It was a war-hammer, with a gold handle and a killing blade of diamonds.

Loki lifted the hammer high above his head, and swept it back. Olaf had no doubt that his next action would be to bring it down on the head of his Uncle Kveld-Ulf. But what Loki hadn't noticed was that by this time, Grimnir had sneaked up behind him. Grimnir wrestled the hammer from the grip of the unfortunate slave. Olaf looked up at his uncle, who once more raised the enormous sword. But catching a glimpse of the bejewelled weapon in Grimnir's hand, he suddenly lost interest in both Olaf and Loki. He stepped across to Grimnir, and grabbed at the hammer. Grimnir yielded it reluctantly, and watched as Kveld-Ulf weighed it, first in his left hand, then in his right. He brandished it above his head and swung it joyously, and then headed back for the longhouse.

'Bring them, and tie them up!' he cried. And many hands grasped at the terrified prisoners.

CHAPTER TOO

'Where is he now?' croaked Hugin.

He was perched on a high-backed settle in the room where the palace servants gathered to toast themselves in front of the log-fire that burned all year round, to warm the thin mountain air.

'Gone to see Jarnsaxa,' said Garram. 'Not that it'll do any good.'

'Who's Jarnsaxa?' asked Hugin, smoothing out his lustrous black wing-feathers with his beak.

'I told you yesterday, you dumb raven. And last week. And the week before.'

'Well, I'm not much good at memory. When Odin wants something remembered, he tells it to Munin. Me, I do thought. Very deep thought. Like just now, for instance, Odin's asked me to think of the whereabouts of a certain someone who's been mysteriously missing from the palace for six months.'

'Oh, you mean . . . ?' asked Garram.

'Exactly.'

'And have you thought where he might be?' asked Garram.

'Well . . . I dunno, I've forgotten who we're talking about now. I'll go and ask Munin later. He's good at remembering things.'

'So anyway,' said Garram, deciding that the conversation was becoming futile, 'like I said, Thor's gone to see Jarnsaxa.'

'Can't do no harm,' Hugin said, hopping onto Garram's shoulder.

'Can't do no harm?' echoed Garram. 'She's a giantess, ain't she? If he mentions it to her . . . '

'Nah, even he wouldn't be that stupid,' Hugin said, cocking his sleek black head on one side. 'By the way, you've got food in your hair.'

'Well, he threw a pie at me,' Garram said. 'You think I've got time to wash my hair every time Thor gets in a bad mood?'

'Very good pie,' said Hugin, appreciatively, as he pecked at the crumbs and strands of meat.

'Made it myself,' Garram said. 'Not that he appreciates it. Two hundred cows' livers went into that pie. Not to mention the onions.'

'Is there any more of this?'

'Swept into a corner in the kitchen. I'll deal with it later.'

'Mind if I go and have a little nibble?'

'Help yourself,' Garram said. 'Listen, you won't say anything about all this, will you? I mean, you won't say anything to . . . ' and here his voice dropped to a whisper, 'you won't say anything to . . . Odin about this. Thor doesn't want him to know.'

'He's busy with his runes at the moment. He wouldn't listen to me even if I did say anything. Not that I will. I mean, obviously it's a bit sensitive, this matter of the . . . of the . . . What exactly were we talking about? It's completely slipped my mind. Anyway, I'll be off to the kitchen for some of that pie.' And with that, Hugin spread his wings, and flew effortlessly down the pillared corridor towards the kitchen.

'Nice that someone appreciates my cooking,' said Garram, to no one in particular, 'even if it's just a raven.'

Two seconds later, Hugin was back.

'Which way's the kitchen?' he asked.

'I told you yesterday, straight down the corridor.'

'Sorry, I forgot.'

And the raven once more fanned his wings and fluttered towards the kitchen. But before he reached the end of the corridor, he wheeled round and glided back to Garram.

'What now?' snappped Garram.

'Sorry, it's just . . . why did I want to go to the kitchen?'

Guarded by Egil and Grimnir, Olaf and Loki sat, roped together at the arms, in a muddy puddle behind the longhouse. Kveld-Ulf had made it clear that he was anxious to try out his new weapon at first light. And both Loki and Olaf were pretty sure who he was going to try it out on.

'Why don't you relax, Egil?' Loki said. 'Scared Kveld-Ulf will find you sitting down on the job?'

'So we can drift off to sleep and let you escape?' said Egil. 'You're not going to catch us that way.' And then Egil winked. Or at least, he closed his left eye. And since that was the only eye he had, it was always difficult to tell whether Egil was winking, or just closing his eye for a moment.

Egil had been on many raids, and had left a bit of himself behind everywhere he went, as a sort of memento for the locals. The little finger of his right hand was somewhere in Frankia, while a couple of the small toes of his right foot had found their everlasting resting place by a picturesque lake where he had encountered an axe-wielding Irish warrior.

Most of Egil's right ear, however, had dropped into a river in Jutland, where he had had a difference of opinion with a Dane who (unfortunately for Egil) had particularly sharp teeth. After twenty years of quarrelling and raiding, Egil hardly had a single limb that was completely intact. As for the missing eye, it was somewhere in Scotland, keeping a look-out (so they said) for native warriors—which was more than it had managed to do when it had been accompanied by the rest of Egil.

A wolf howled, lonely, in the distance. There was a sudden breeze, and the trees gave a rustling rush of excitement. Egil, who had been jigging up and down for some time, shuffled off to a bush at the edge of the enclosure.

Olaf looked at Loki, hopelessly, and Loki looked back, and said:

'Remember the Jomsvikings.' He said it without moving his lips. In fact, if it hadn't been Loki's unmistakable, fluting voice, Olaf would have assumed that the sound came from Grimnir, or Egil.

'Remember the what?' he hissed.

But Egil was back now.

'No talking, or I'll have to take your heads off,' he said.

There was a long silence. Egil looked sympathet-ically at Olaf.

'When a glacier sees the spring sun, he weeps,' he said.

Olaf wasn't sure what to make of this, but nod-ded sagely. Egil had always been fond of obscure proverbs.

'It is impossible to be the friend of everyone for long, is a true proverb,' Egil added.

Olaf nodded. Egil nodded.

Grimnir chimed in. 'When a boy's skull is split open, his brains come out. Also a true proverb,' he said, and laughed hugely.

Olaf pulled at the ropes that secured him to Loki. The knots looked fiendishly complicated.

Grimnir followed his gaze, and grinned.

'I wouldn't bother if I were you. That's a triple half shark-hitch. You'll pull your arm off before you get it free. In fact, go on, pull your arm off, I could do with a bit of a laugh.'

Olaf stared Grimnir full in the face, until he looked away, and then tried the ropes once more. And in his head, he tried to recall what Loki had said. Remember the Jomsvikings. The Jomsvikings.

It did sound familiar. Some story his father had told him, in the long-ago, before he sailed off, never to return. Olaf drifted to sleep, and when he opened his eyes, the purple of the sky to the east was lightening. Already, people were slowly spilling out of the longhouse, and soon, Kveld-Ulf was approaching, purposefully swinging the mighty battle-hammer.

In a panic, Olaf sprang to his feet, dragging Loki with him, and began to head for the enclosure fence. Unfortunately, this meant that Loki had to run backwards—and he was clearly not very skilled in this, for he was soon tumbling in the mud, taking Olaf with him. There were bellows of laughter from men and women who were now sleepily bumbling around the enclosure. Grimnir and Egil simply moved over to where the pair had collapsed, and waited, smiling, their swords still drawn.

'I can't kill my own nephew,' Kveld-Ulf announced. 'It wouldn't be right. Egil, you do it.' And he handed over to Egil the mighty war-hammer that had been snatched from Loki the day before. Once more, Olaf tried to remember the Jomsvikings. And suddenly, the whole thing came back in an instant.

The Jomsvikings of Denmark had unwisely picked a fight with the army of King Hakon of

Norway, and been not only defeated, but wiped out, annihilated, whipped, beaten into a smooth cream and then spread over the local countryside like butter over a warm piece of bread. The few survivors were rounded up to be beheaded.

But the first Jomsviking said to the executioner:

'My hair hasn't fought against you. Please hold it back when you chop off my head.'

The executioner agreed, twisting the man's long hair in his hands, and then swiping his deadly axe at the Jomsviking's neck. But at the last moment, the Jomsviking pulled his head forward, so that the executioner's axe missed its mark and dug itself into his own leg. The other Danes were so amused by the trick that they agreed to let the prisoners go free.

When Olaf realized what Loki had meant, he felt bitterly disappointed. Was this the best idea he could come up with? Was it likely that Olaf would have enough strength to make a big man like Egil miss his mark?

Egil looked down at Olaf.

'A one-armed man is better than a corpse,' he said. 'A corpse is no use to anyone. I thought that might be of comfort to you.'

'Thanks.'

'Is it of comfort to you?'

'No, but thanks anyway,' said Olaf.

'Actually, now I come to think of it, that proverb is for comforting people with one arm, rather than people who are going to have their head smashed in.'

'Yes, but the thought was there.'

'Where do you think?' Egil asked, politely. 'Back of the head, or front?'

'Either way's fine,' Olaf replied, equally politely.

'Only I always find that with the front of the head, it messes up the face. Whereas I've known times when I've smashed in the back of someone's head and hardly done any damage at all.' He paused, thoughtfully. 'Apart from them being dead, that is. And the fact that their brains go all over the . . .'

'Just get on with it, would you?' Olaf said, getting just a touch impatient.

Egil lifted the hammer, but hesitated for a moment. It was then that Olaf decided to give Loki's idea a try.

'Actually, I'll go for the back, if that's OK,' Olaf said.

Egil shrugged, and nodded.

'And if you could just hold my hair out of the

23

way. I don't want it all matted with blood if I get to the Valholl.'

Egil grasped Olaf's hair, and wound it round the two remaining fingers of his left hand. Then he grasped the hammer between the thumb and two and a half fingers which were left on his right hand, and brought it down.

Olaf left it late. Very late. As he jerked forwards, the hammer grazed the skin at the back of his neck. It continued its swing downwards until it connected with Egil's left foot. One of the wedge-shaped diamonds on the head connected with his boot, and took out a neat little triangle from the tip. Egil stood silently for a moment, then bent and picked up the piece of boot. He turned it upside down and out dropped a toe. That was when Egil started to wail.

Egil howled and yowled. He gibbered and jabbered and jumped on the spot. Apart from the pain, he was feeling very miffed. Left-foot toes were the last thing he had a complete set of. And of course, the whole village shrieked with laughter. Olaf saw his moment. Egil had sheathed his sword to wield the mighty hammer, and—with Egil bent double—that placed it just at Olaf's eye level. Olaf grasped the sword handle and pulled. Suddenly, he felt stronger than he had ever felt before. Grasping the hilt of the sword with both hands, he swung it round in a deadly arc that had Egil limping off towards the longhouse in terror. Instead of running away, Olaf went forwards, forwards, aiming blow after blow at his hairy assailants, who scattered, half in surprise, half in terror. It couldn't last, of course. Eventually he was tripped from behind and found himself sprawling in the dirt, and hands wrested the sword from his grasp.

Egil limped back to Olaf and raised the hammer.

'Just get on with it!' roared Kveld-Ulf.

'That's right,' said Loki, 'kill him, quick. He's a berserk. You don't want him doing all the fighting for you and grabbing the glory. Much better to die yourselves and get to the Valholl.'

'A berserk,' mused Kveld-Ulf. 'I've always said, you can't beat a good berserk. We'll take him with us. But you can kill the slave.'

'Wait!' said Loki. 'Do you intend chopping my head off my body, or my body off my head?'

'Well, both, I suppose,' said Egil.

'What, you mean you're going to kill me twice? That's hardly fair, now is it?'

Egil lowered the hammer, and scratched his chin, trying to think it through. He was not the brightest of Vikings, and hadn't been able to count above six since he'd lost four of his fingers.

Suddenly, Kveld-Ulf roared with laughter, obviously amused by the spectacle of the perplexed Egil.

'That slave could talk the sea out of a fjord. We'll take him with us too. Let no one say I can't be merciful when the occasion demands it.'

'I could carry that heavy hammer for you,' Loki said, and reached out to Egil for the beautiful weapon.

'Keep your thieving stinking slave hands off it!' bawled Ulf. And Loki retreated, reluctantly, to join the queue of men who were now lumbering towards the ship. Every fit man in the village had joined the line. That is, every fit man except Grimnir, who hung back, close to Kveld-Ulf.

'Perhaps it would be best,' he wheedled, 'if I stayed behind to look after the place in your absence.'

'All right,' growled Kveld-Ulf. 'But if things aren't in good order when I return, you'll wish that you'd risked your neck with the rest of us.'

CHAPTER THREE

'You've never seen our ship, have you, Loki?'

'No. In case you've forgotten, I've been tied to a post for the last six months. But I have to say, I'm looking forward to it. It's a good while since I've seen a fine longship . . . '

That was when they reached the bay, and caught sight of the *Skuldelev*.

'It's not actually a longship. It's a knarr,' Olaf explained.

'Oh,' said Loki.

'It's a trading vessel, really. You can shift a lot of seal blubber in one of these things. Of course, they've had to patch the bow a bit,' said Olaf.

'So I see.'

'Also the stern.'

'Right.'

'And the midship section needs a bit of work, really, when you look at it.'

'So, what you are telling me is that having spent six interminable months grovelling in mud and tied to a post, I'm going to sea in a pile of patched-up wood-shavings with a mast on the top,' said Loki.

'You see, my father went off in the village long-ship six years ago,' Olaf said.

'Didn't anyone think of . . . building another one?'

'Kveld-Ulf's not big on boat-building,' Olaf explained. 'He's more keen on stuff like belching and drinking.'

'Do you think if I asked nicely,' Loki sighed, 'they'd just hit us with the hammer and get it over with?'

Olaf was one of the first to board. He sprawled, exhausted, in the stern. The lack of sleep, the fear, and the energy spent in his frenzied attack on Kveld-Ulf's men had left him puffy-eyed and longing to lie down somewhere—anywhere—and it was through half-closed eyes that he watched the rest of the crew coming aboard. The rope was cast off and the tide began to take the ship out into the waters of the Scagerrak, and soon the crew began rowing. Two men to each oar, and pulling furiously, they were moving as fast as the old tub was likely to go, with much splashing as the crew got back into practice after a long winter spent ashore. Olaf staggered to his feet and hung on to the side, as his old life slipped away over the horizon. He watched until the village, the woods, the fjord, were swallowed by the sea. Then he lay at the bottom of the ship, and dropped into sleep.

Olaf was awoken by a gentle kick in the leg. He had been sleeping on his side, and when he opened his eyes, he could see that the deliverer of the kick was Harald.

'We need bailers,' Harald said with a grin. It was true. They had only been at sea a couple of hours, but already there was a large, rolling puddle along the bottom of the boat. Olaf reached for the leathern bucket that hung from the mast, then scooped up some of the water. To get it over the top-strake meant clambering up the side of the ship and tipping the bucket into the waves. Harald watched him for a while, laughing to himself at Olaf's efforts. Then he turned his attentions to Loki.

'Oi, slave!' he said, delivering a hefty kick. 'Bailing time.'

Loki stirred unwillingly, evidently emerging from a deep and comfortable sleep. Olaf had noticed before that he seemed to have a cat-like ability to relax anywhere. Loki picked up a bucket, but didn't seem in any hurry to do any actual work. He leaned against the side, bucket in hand, until Egil limped up.

'Why aren't you working, slave? "It is a foolish man who owns no ox, and pulls the plough himself" . . . or should that be, "a foolish man owns an ox and . . . " Well, never mind about proverbs. Why aren't you working?'

'I'm so sorry,' Loki said, 'I've never done this sort of thing before. I'm not sure how you do it.'

'Not sure how to . . . well, you just dip in your bucket and you . . . and you bail!' Egil bellowed.

'Yes, but perhaps being an old sea-faring man, you just don't realize how many skills you have at your fingertips. It might come naturally to you, it's far from simple for a humble slave like me,' said Loki. 'Tell you what, perhaps you could show me.'

'Well, all right. You dip your bucket in like this.'

'Ah, so you scoop with the *open* end of the bucket. I would have got that wrong for a start. That is so clever. And what do you do next?'

'Well, you kind of scoop. Pull it along the water, until some of it goes into the bucket. And then you tip it over the side.'

'That is ingenious,' said Loki. 'You couldn't show me again, could you? I didn't quite get it the first time.'

'Well, all right,' said Egil. 'Scoop first.'

'Using the open end of the bucket?'

'Exactly,' said Egil. 'Now let me show you a few times, and I think you'll get the idea.'

And Egil continued, with Loki's encouragement, bailing hard. Harald watched, and seemed on the point of intervening, but then he smiled to himself, winked at Olaf, and enjoyed the spectacle of Egil unwittingly doing exactly what he was told by the slave Loki. Then Harald opened the lid of his sea-chest and pulled out a small leather pouch. He offered it to Olaf.

'You'll need this.' And he handed Olaf a short sword—battered and rusty, but just the right weight and size for Olaf to use. He held it, experimentally, and swept it back and forth a couple of times.

Some time later, Olaf noticed that several of the men had gathered around Kveld-Ulf.

'A storm. Sure as anything,' Harald was saying, 'and coming this way. A day or two will make no difference. We need to shelter.'

'Coward!' Kveld-Ulf screamed into his face. 'Pink-kneed son of a moon-faced tripe-eating pile of fetid walrus-blubber!'

Harald stood his ground, and his hand strayed to the hilt of his sword.

'My sun-compass says we're nearer to Denmark than Shetland,' he said.

'Well,' said Ulf, swinging a cruel punch at the side of Harald's head, 'my fist says we go on.' Harald sprawled full-length in the bottom of the ship, and Ulf returned to his place at the prow.

Olaf was very uneasy about this new situation. Harald was never wrong about weather. Soon the rain came. Huge half-frozen droplets hurled against face and hands. Harald, Loki, and Egil took in the sail, then pointed the bow to windward, and in deafening wind and near blackness, they rode out the storm. Waves broke over the bow, big enough to replace all the water that had been bailed in the last hour with a single deluge. Soon, all were bailing, using helmets, buckets, wooden beakers, and even bare hands, desperately scooping and flinging out the water, but still the spray and the waves piled over the top-strakes, until the crew were sloshing around up to their freezing knees in salt water.

At any moment it seemed the ship might be overwhelmed as wave after wave crashed against it. With each wave, the patched strakes came further apart from the hull. Then Loki started behaving very strangely. He worked his way along the ship, and at each crack and gap, he muttered a few words, and touched the splitting timber. The strange thing was that when the waves battered again, instead of opening further, they closed in, fusing together like magic. Only Olaf saw this— everyone else was too busy bailing or steering or steadying the ship with the oars.

The ship was now lying so low in the water that at times Olaf was convinced that the next wave would take them to the bottom of the sea, but somehow the frantic crew kept her afloat. The storm raged on, but the men worked with a will as Olaf clung miserably to the mast.

Then Olaf saw a speck. Just a little black dot, perched on the sea on the very edge of the horizon. When he looked again it was gone. Perhaps he had imagined it. Or perhaps he was just imagining that he'd imagined it, because when he looked again, it was still there. He squealed. It was all he had the energy to do, to squeal and point. Harald looked. And he said one word.

'Shetland.'

CHAPTER FOUR

Olaf pulled himself over the top-strake, and fell onto the stone-built jetty, then staggered along it to land. In front of him was Kveld-Ulf. Loki loped closely behind. The rest of the crew followed, too exhausted to be thankful for their miraculous escape. Some twenty or thirty people had come to gawp at the newly arrived ship, and when they saw the state of it, the reaction was hilarity.

An old man detached himself from the crowd and approached them. He possessed the biggest beard Olaf had ever seen. It was a beard of monstrous proportions. It projected outwards in all directions, concealing the neck and ears, and stretched up to the wild, white eyebrows, whose bristles flailed out in all directions, as if trying to escape. He could only imagine that some kind of human being was attached to the back end of this gargantuan collection of whiskers, but it was difficult to see where.

'Today you are the guests of Snorri the Boneless,'

he said, in a strange Danish accent. 'Only the best for men who have been brave enough to venture out in that.' (Here he gestured at the ship.) 'I'll take you somewhere you'll truly feel at home.'

And so they began to march across the island. Kveld-Ulf walked ahead with the bearded man, with Loki and Olaf following close behind.

Kveld-Ulf turned and addressed the beard.

'How much?' he asked, flatly.

'Oh, let's not argue about that. I'm not much of a businessman, I'm sure you'll do very well out of old Snorri.'

'How much?' repeated Kveld-Ulf.

'Well, there's a mooring-fee, and then a charge for accommodation, plus food, for thirty-two people—I hadn't really given it a thought, but I'd say perhaps, just in round figures, two hundred and fifty-six Arabic shekels, or sixty-eight Frankish sous, or eighty-two drachmas . . . '

For answer, Kveld-Ulf produced a silver bar from a bag slung at his waist, and snapped it in the middle.

'This is what you're getting,' he growled, handing over half the silver. 'Take it or leave it.'

'Is that all? You want to rob a poor old Dane, stuck here freezing and lonely all year long? You're going to cut poor old Snorri's profit to the bone?'

'Well, that was the general idea,' said Kveld-Ulf, 'now where are you taking us?'

Snorri mutely pointed the way, and Kveld-Ulf strode off ahead.

'Would you like to hear the story,' Snorri said, pocketing the silver, and turning to Loki and Olaf, 'of how Vollklung the Brave saved his longship from being pounded to splinters on the rocky coast of Iceland?'

Snorri had such a droning, monotonous voice that already Olaf could feel sleep tugging at his eyelids.

'No thank you,' said Olaf.

'Yes please,' said Loki.

'Really?' droned the beard. 'Are you sure? Most people don't, you see. But then they're an ignorant lot round here. I'll tell it to you as we walk along. "Vollklung the Brave was returning from a long voyage . . . "'

'Wonderful, wonderful. Very exciting,' Loki said. 'But what I meant was, I was wondering if you would like to entertain our crew tonight. They're very fond of stories. Perhaps you have some really long saga. Our men are always ready to listen to an interesting story-teller like you.'

'Well, I'd be delighted,' said the beard, 'I'll be there at nightfall.'

And with this, Snorri bumbled off to catch up with Kveld-Ulf.

'What exactly are you up to?' demanded Olaf, as soon as Snorri was out of earshot.

'Me?' protested Loki, all innocence. 'I just thought a bit of exciting story-telling might entertain us after a tedious voyage in that mouldy heap of rotting timber that your people call a boat.'

Quite soon, they saw a welcome sight ahead. It was a longhouse—exactly the same size and shape as those at home—the same turf roof, but with walls of stone.

There was a cheerful blaze inside, and an enormous table spread with trenchers of meat and bread and fish. The bedraggled sailors sat at the benches and began guzzling the warm wine and pulling at the meat. Olaf chewed suspiciously on a piece of lamb. Or it might have been beef. Or maybe actually it was herring. It was difficult to tell, because it was definitely past its best. All you could tell was that it was either a piece of fish that tasted vaguely of meat, or a piece of meat that tasted vaguely of fish. He poured a drink into a wooden cup, and sipped. This was off too. It was either cider that tasted a bit like beer, or beer that tasted a bit like cider.

'What do you think?' Snorrie intoned. 'Isn't it nice to have such good food and drink after your difficult voyage?'

'Call this food?' said Kveld-Ulf, still chewing. 'I'd throw it to the dogs, if you had any dogs. Which you don't. You probably killed them all with this disgusting muck.'

Kveld-Ulf had placed the hammer, wrapped in its ragged bit of leather, at his feet. Olaf looked from the hammer to Loki's face.

'Where did the hammer come from?' he asked, quietly.

Loki didn't hear the question. Or at least, he pretended not to.

When everyone had eaten their fill, and found warm corners to sprawl in, Loki said:

'With your permission, Kveld-Ulf, Snorri has kindly offered to tell us a saga.'

'Is he charging us any extra for it?'

'No,' Loki said, 'it's completely free. An unmissable opportunity. Snorri is a famous teller of sagas.'

Kveld made a gesture of assent, and Snorri began:

'Ketil Flatneb was a famous warrior in Norway. He was the son of Bjorn Rough-foot . . .'

Harald stifled a yawn, in a desperate battle to stay awake, then slumped backwards, and emitted a huge snore. Snorri continued, oblivious:

'His wife was Yngvild, daughter of Svein Wether . . . '

Then Olaf felt a yawn rising like an unstoppable sea-monster. He pushed it down, and clenched his teeth together.

' . . . their daughters were Auth the Deep-minded, Thorun the Horned, and Jorun Manwitbrent . . . '

When Olaf woke again, the old Dane was still talking, but could barely be heard for the chorus of snores that rang out from every corner of the room. Olaf guessed that Snorri had been telling the story for a good while, but he hadn't finished the introduction yet:

'Also their cousins, whose two sons were Thorvald Green-Eye and Amlet Smoothface, whose daughter, Afnar, was given as bride to Habsnad of Sweden . . . '

Olaf opened his eyes, and saw that the only person moving around the room—indeed the only person now awake apart from Olaf and Snorri—was Loki, who was quietly approaching the unconscious body of Kveld-Ulf. Gingerly, Loki reached for the bundle in which the hammer was kept, and pulled back the leather, revealing a ruby the size of an eyeball. He stooped down, as if to grab the hammer.

In a very short time, a number of thoughts went through Olaf's head. The first thought was that if Loki were caught trying to take the hammer, then there would be a good deal of trouble. The second was that if Loki did steal it, and somehow managed to escape from the island with it, then Kveld-Ulf would pursue him relentlessly until it was recovered, which might mean that Olaf would never get a chance to search for his father.

Olaf sat up, and said, loudly, 'So, this Thorvald Green-Eye was the grandson of the second husband of the wife of Ketil Flatneb?'

Snorri was startled. No one had ever interrupted one of his sagas to ask him a question before. This was largely because no one had actually ever listened to one of his stories for more than fifteen seconds without falling asleep.

'No,' he said, irritated. 'Thorvald was son of Haakon One-Eye, and grandson of Svilt Hijkson and of Svein the Black.'

'Oh, sorry,' said Olaf, loudly. 'Carry on.'

Olaf's interruption had woken many of the sleepers, and Loki crept away from Ulf, trying (and failing) to look like someone who hadn't been attempting to steal the hammer.

'Where was I?' said Snorri, who had completely lost his thread now. 'Oh, never mind, I'll start again.'

'Ketil Flatneb was a famous warrior in Norway. He was the son of Bjorn Rough-foot . . .'

At first light, Olaf woke, and breakfasted on cold meat and weak beer from the supper table, then began to walk back to Helli Ness, the bay where the *Skuldelev* was moored. It was calm now. Blue skies, a low watery sun, and a sea creased with little wavelets. Olaf was just thinking how pleasant it was to spend some time on his own, when he heard Loki's voice behind him.

'I have to go back,' Loki said. 'It's vital. It's essential. And what's more . . . ' Loki put a hand on Olaf's shoulder, ' . . . it's very, very important,' he continued, confidentially.

'Why?'

'Can't tell you. But I must get back to Norway. If I'd known your ships could sail against the wind, I'd never have got on the boat in the first place. I thought we'd be blown straight back again in a couple of hours.'

'Of course they can sail against the wind. You wouldn't get very far if you had to wait for a wind blowing in exactly the right direction. It's called tacking. Even I know that, and I've never sailed a boat outside the fjord back home.'

By now they had reached the jetty where the old *Skuldelev* was wallowing low in the water, looking more like a half-demolished privy than a ship. Moored to another jetty was a neat little fishing-boat, with mast and sail neatly stowed in the bottom.

'Olaf, you have to help me,' Loki said, calmly. 'We're going to steal the hammer, and then find a way of getting back to Norway.'

'Are you mad?' squealed Olaf. 'If you steal that hammer, then my uncle will be after you. Apart from which, I don't want to go to Norway. I'm going to Angle-land to find my father.'

'Shhh!' hissed Loki, urgently. He pointed over to the jetty. Some of the crew had begun to arrive. Harald leapt over the top-strake of the *Skuldelev*, waist-deep in the icy water. He gave a high-pitched squeal in response to the biting cold. All laughed, and then more men joined him in the ship.

Soon, there was a relay of crewmen bailing her out. Buckets were passed along from the bottom of the ship to men sitting astride the top-strakes, who emptied them out into the sea. The more they bailed, the more amazed they were that they had got the boat to harbour.

Kveld-Ulf, of course, did not play a large part in actually doing the repair work. He staggered up some time after everyone else, and sat sunning himself on the front-deck. He had brought with him a jar of wine, and a wooden cup. He put them down on the deck next to him. He also put down the hammer on the boards, and couldn't resist peeling back the leather cover to reveal the exquisite jewels which studded the handle and blade.

Loki stood on the jetty next to the ship, eyeing the jewels that flashed in the sunlight through the opening in the hammer's cover. He took a careful step onto the upper front-deck of the *Skuldelev*, so stealthily that no one felt any movement as he crept on board. Then he jumped back in shock as two enormous ravens landed, squawking, inches away from him. All heads swivelled round now. The ravens seemed very interested in the hammer. One had pulled at the leather cover with his beak, and the other was hopping around the thing—now landing on the handle, now pecking experimentally at it, now moving his head slowly from side to side.

Loki turned for a moment to look at the new arrivals, then stepped nimbly down into the flooded mid-ship section, and stood next to a bucket. Olaf watched him, curiously. It was as if he was trying to make himself inconspicuous. But why would Loki want to hide from a couple of grubby old ravens?

Olaf looked to the front of the vessel again. One of the ravens seemed for a moment to have forgotten about the hammer. It made a dive down into the bottom part of the ship to pick up a dried herring that was floating around in the bilge-water. Then he flew back to join his comrade. When Olaf looked around to see what Loki was up to this time, he was gone. But Olaf could have sworn that last time he'd looked, there had just been one bucket there. Now there were two. And curiously enough, one of the buckets reminded him of Loki. This was odd, because normally Loki looked nothing like a bucket. Olaf looked carefully at the thing. The rope-handle was vaguely the same colour as Loki's flaxen hair, and there was a bump halfway up the bucket's side that looked a little like an elfin nose, but that was where the resemblance ended. Olaf rubbed his eyes. It must be the lack of sleep, or something—he was imagining things. Egil flapped his cloak at the ravens, and they flew into the air, cawing loudly.

'They're dirty,' said Kveld-Ulf, 'they steal, and they fly at the first sign of danger. They'd fit in really well in this crew.'

The crew laughed, and returned to their business, and that was when Olaf realized that Loki was there after all—must have been there all along, because there he was, skulking behind the mast, trying to look busy, turning a piece of splintered wood in his hands and examining it seriously.

There was much rushing around and hammering, and pulling at damaged timber. Olaf was given the job of stuffing wads of animal hair into the joins between the strakes. Harald lit a fire, using a burning stick brought from one of the little houses, and on the fire he set an iron pot. Olaf wondered if this was to be lunch, until the foul smell drifted over to him.

'Seal-tar,' Harald explained, and placed the pot next to the vessel. Olaf knew without being told what he had to do with it, and began transferring the disgusting liquid into the hair-stuffed cracks. In the process, he also transferred it to his eyelids, hair, ears, and nose.

CHAPTER FIVE

'How's he handling it?' Hugin asked, pecking at a dish of choice meat-scraps. 'Better now?'

'He's off his food,' said Garram.

'Is he? That's not like him,' cawed Munin, cocking his head sideways to keep an eye on Hugin, who was greedily lifting his head, and shaking his beak to guzzle down a large piece of meat. 'He's only missed three meals in the last two hundred and fifty years.'

'How do you remember all that stuff?' said Hugin.

'What do you mean?' asked Munin.

'All that stuff about . . . whatever it was you was just remembering,' Hugin said, vaguely. 'Anyway, the power of deep thought has come to Thor's aid. Some days ago, I came up with a plan.'

'What plan?' Garram asked.

'It was a corker. My plan, devised with all the power of my powerful deep thinking brain was . . . Well, what I decided to do was . . . I had this amazing plan, which was . . . What was my plan, Munin?'

'Hugin's plan,' said Munin, 'was to harness the power of flight. We would fly over every inch of ground and ocean north and south, east and west. That's why we're so hungry, you see. We flew all over the world, searching.'

'And did you find it?' said Garram.

'Yes,' croaked Munin.

'Don't tell me,' said Garram, 'Hugin found it, but he can't remember where.'

'No, no, no. We went together. That was all part of the plan. Otherwise, Hugin would have forgotten what he was looking for before he even left the palace.'

'So,' said Garram, excitedly. 'Can you tell me where you found it?'

'Yes,' Munin said. 'I can tell you exactly where it was.'

'Well, go on then.'

'It was wrapped in leather. Leather made from the skin of a goat. There was a little stain on the top right-hand corner of the leather. It was on a piece of wood with a large knot in it, and the wood was split just above the knot. This piece of wood was joined to another piece of wood, also

48

with a knot in it. And next to the hammer was a jar of wine. And a wooden cup. So there, you see,' Munin said, smugly, 'we know exactly where it is. All that I lodged in my memory.'

'Is that all you committed to your memory?'

'Yes.'

'And you didn't commit to your memory whether it was on a table or in a house or on a ship or on land or on sea or in the east or the west or the north or the south?'

'No.'

'Why not?'

'I didn't think.'

Olaf and Loki were the last to make their way back from the ship, since they had been given the job of tidying up after the repair work. They were both ravenously hungry when they arrived at the house. The smell of roasted food that drifted out of the doorway promised a much better meal than they had eaten the night before. Sure enough, the table was groaning with freshly roasted joints of meat, and fresh bread and fruit. Olaf and Loki stood in the doorway for a few seconds, breathing in the delicious smell. Then Kveld-Ulf spoke.

'Slave! Over here.'

Unwillingly, Loki walked over to where Kveld-Ulf was standing with Snorri.

'This is the one,' Kveld Ulf said, 'a good strong slave. Young, too. I think you've got yourself a bargain.'

'You've sold me?' gasped Loki, in disbelief.

'I said I would, if you gave me trouble. Did you really think I hadn't noticed you trying to steal my hammer? Egil, get the shackles.'

Grinning, Egil picked up some rusty iron from the floor.

'I want him well and truly restrained, mind,' warbled Snorri.

'But, Kveld-Ulf, why?' asked Loki. 'You need me. I can help you.'

'You and that good-for-nothing nephew of mine have been plotting ever since we boarded back in Skirringsvijk.'

'The head stuck on a plot no longer pikes,' Egil said. 'I mean, "the head stuck on a pike no longer plots". That's a proverb, you know.'

'You can't sell him!' exclaimed Olaf.

'Well, strictly speaking, we're not,' said Kveld-Ulf. 'We're swapping him for a good meal and a little fishing boat. If you keep your mouth shut, you can have some of the food. If you don't we'll sell you as well.'

'You mustn't,' blustered Loki. 'You can't sell me.' He pulled himself up to his full height. 'Do you know who I *am*?'

The Vikings were very amused by his self-importance, and howled with laughter.

Egil began to slip one of the iron shackles around Loki's leg.

At that moment, there was a deafening roar outside. It was the sound of many men, screaming for blood. Added to that was the sound of swords, beating on shields. And then the thud of running feet, the neighing of horses. The door shook and the whole room echoed with the sound of a battleaxe sinking itself into the heavy timber. All stood, astonished for a moment, trying to work out what was happening. How could so many men and horses have arrived so suddenly on Shetland? There were more screams from outside, followed by the sound of another battleaxe sinking into the timbers of the door.

Egil dropped the shackle with a loud clank. Snorri's beard shook with fear. Kveld-Ulf got up to look through a crack in the door.

'Can't see them—they must be over the brow of

the hill,' he pronounced. 'But it sounds like there's a big army out there.'

He drew his sword, and lunged back to pick up the hammer. But the hammer was gone. With a scream of rage, he stamped around, bellowing. Olaf felt a powerful tug at his elbow, which propelled him out of the door, and he found himself outside, being dragged along by Loki. When Olaf glanced backwards, he could see one or two men peeping gingerly through the doorway, but none dared to face the huge army that must have produced such a terrifying noise. The sound was getting closer now. Mixed with the clashing of metal, and the angry roar of men, there were also the hoofbeats of mighty war-horses. He stopped for a moment, but then Loki continued to pull him towards the sound. He yielded, unwillingly, and allowed himself to be dragged off.

And so they continued. Loki, who seemed suddenly to have superhuman strength, propelled him headlong towards the terrible noise of the approaching hordes. Onward they ran, all the way back to the jetty. Loki ran straight past the *Skuldelev*, and leapt into the tiny fishing boat which was moored to the next jetty. Without thinking, Olaf dived in after him, and found himself sitting, gasping, in the bottom of the boat, a little like a fish that has just been hauled out of the sea, and flaps around, wondering what kind of terrifying world it has been hoisted into. Loki fiddled ineffectually with the knots in the mooring-rope.

'What are you doing?' said Olaf. 'Where do you think you're . . . '

Loki held up the hammer and, suddenly, Olaf realized Loki's intentions.

'I'm not going to Norway with you, Loki.'

'No time to argue. Knots. I've never been able to undo knots. You have to do this for me.'

'But, Loki, I'm going to Angle-land to find my father.'

'Of course you are. Just as soon as you've taken me back to Norway.'

'I won't. I shan't. My uncle Kveld is going to Angle-land. It's not my fault you're a slave. He can sell you if he wants. I'm going to go to Angle-land on the *Skuldelev*.'

'You think he's really going to let you look for your father?'

'Well,' said Olaf, 'he might. And this little tub won't make it all the way back to Norway. Even you must realize that. You're on your own, Loki.'

'But, Olaf, I need you. I don't do sailing. Usually I live high up in the hills. You'd be surprised how infrequently I've found myself having to get into a boat on top of a mountain. Please, Olaf, you must help me. You know about rigging and knots and . . . and ticking . . . '

'Tacking,' Olaf corrected.

'You see? I can't even get the right *word* for it. You must come with me.'

Of course, Olaf could have just jumped out of the boat and let him get on with it. But he couldn't help feeling concerned for Loki, who knew nothing about sailing and would obviously drown before he even got out of the bay. With a heavy heart, he undid the painter. He knew exactly how to pull the rope in order to release the boat, and soon he was rowing out into the bay, as Loki fumbled with the sail. The crew were now approaching the jetty, with Kveld-Ulf at their head, brandishing a shining battleaxe.

Olaf tried to scream a warning, but his voice was folded into the shushing of the sea, and the shouts of the crew.

'Trust me,' Loki said, struggling with the tangled sail, 'just do what I . . . '

But that was all he said, because at that moment

there was a loud thump, which propelled him forward. With a muffled cry, Loki slid down the mast and lay in a curled heap, with blood welling from the gash made by the axe deeply embedded in his back.

CHAPTER SIX

Olaf let the boat drift for a moment, and crouched down beside the stricken Loki, whose breath gurgled in and out painfully. Suddenly, more axes were flying through the air, bouncing off the sides of the little boat and splashing into the sea. A spear flew past, close to Olaf's cheek. Then things became quiet. Kveld's crew were standing on the jetty, watching.

Olaf looked across the water at Kveld-Ulf, who was visibly trembling with rage. It was time for Olaf to make a choice. If he went back, then there was just a chance that Kveld-Ulf would be so grateful for the return of the hammer that he would forgive all. On the other hand, he could head out for the open sea, which would be almost certain death to a boy who had never before sailed beyond the narrow confines of his own fjord. He looked down again at poor Loki, who was now barely able to breathe. And he decided then and there that Kveld-Ulf would not have the hammer.

He began to row, furiously, and there was another little flurry of spears, one of which embedded itself in the side of the boat. When he was out of range, he let the boat drift once more, and tugged the axe from Loki's back. The wound was a gaping mess. Flesh was mixed with bits of rib, and blood welled up into the wound. His tunic was slowly turning from green to sodden scarlet. Loki was still breathing, but there was nothing Olaf could do for him.

Back on the quay, Olaf could see that Kveld-Ulf's crew were jumping onto the *Skuldelev*. She wasn't completely repaired, but Olaf calculated that it wouldn't take long to patch her up, and when they did, they would easily out-pace the little sailing-boat. Olaf looked down once more at the gaping wound on Loki's back. And suddenly, miraculously, the wound started to close. At first, Olaf wondered if it was his imagination, but as he mopped up the blood with the hem of Loki's tunic, it seemed as if the shattered ribs were knitting together before his eyes; one by one, the broken ends finding each other, and then fusing. Muscle and flesh began to bond, until the open wound became a red gash, and the red gash became a long gouge, and the long gouge became a scratch, and the scratch disappeared and all there was to show for the terrible wound was a red mark on the white flesh. And in a moment this vanished too, leaving only the torn fabric to show that anything had happened. Loki roused himself and sat up.

'Will you stop staring at me?' he said. 'I'm having a bad enough day as it is.'

For a while, neither of them had energy for conversation. Olaf took to the oars again, in a frantic effort to put some distance between them and Kveld-Ulf. Finally, mercifully, Olaf felt a whisper of breeze against his face. He shipped the oars, and raised the sail, which tugged the boat effortlessly out to sea. Loki sprawled against the side of the boat, with his head on the top-strake, and Olaf settled back in the keel.

'So?' said Olaf, when he had finally got his breath back.

'What?' Loki groaned.

'So how do you recover from a fatal wound in ten seconds?'

'I'll tell you later.'

'I want to know now,' Olaf hissed. 'I want to know where that hammer came from, and . . . and who managed to make a noise like a thousand men when there was no one there, and . . . '

'I'll answer in a riddle. It will give you something to think about during the voyage.'

'I don't want a riddle,' protested Olaf, 'I want answers.'

But Loki ignored him:

'Look at my hands: the hands of a thief
Less than a man: but more than a man
Hear my name: the name of a trickster
Less than a god: but more than a god
My body was made between earth and Asgard
Steel cannot cleave my flesh.'

'Don't talk rubbish, Loki. I want answers.'

Loki pulled his cloak around his shoulders, and closed his eyes. 'It's all there if you'll just think,' he said. 'Now I need to sleep.' And he settled back, and his breathing became regular. Olaf looked down at the sleeping body. He could have kicked Loki, but after all he had had a pretty rough time. It's not every day you have a battleaxe embedded in your back. So Olaf let him be, and concentrated on steering the little boat through the choppy waves.

But the words of the riddle ran round and round his head, and mingled with the flap of the sail and the creak of the timbers and the slap of the spray.

* * *

'Any luck, majesty?' Garram enquired.

'What do you think?'

'I don't know, Your Thorship, I'm sure it's none of my business. Can I get you a roasted ox or two, for a little snack?'

'I don't want to eat,' Thor thundered.

'Some beer then? Mead? Wine? Ale? How about some cider? We're a bit short at the moment, but I could probably manage to rustle up ten or eleven bucketfuls if I have a good look round. Just to wet your whistle, like.'

'I don't want to drink.'

'Any sign of Loki? Maybe he'd have some ideas.'

'Loki's gone. Disappeared. Haven't seen him for months. I've decided to ask everyone in the palace. All the servants. The trolls in the boiler-room, the dwarves in the workshop.'

'I'm not sure that's a good idea.'

'Oh, don't worry, I'll ask them nicely.'

'But, Your Thorship, remember when you lost your belt? And you thought Alfrigg might have it, and went down to ask him nicely where it was?'

'Oh, yes. How is Alfrigg?'

'Well, the splints are off now, but he's still limping.'

'All right, Garram, what do you suggest?' Thor asked, with a dangerous touch of irritation in his voice.

'You have to go and tell Odin. Now it's gone, we're all in deadly danger from marauding giants. Odin has to know.'

'Tell Odin!' roared Thor. 'What kind of idiot would suggest a stupid idea like that?'

'What kind of idiot would lose the most important weapon in Asgard? Now, Thor, I didn't mean it to come out like that. It was nothing personal. Violence will get you nowhere, Your Thorship. No, please. Thor, please put the cupboard down . . . '

'Are we nearly there yet?' whined Loki.

'For the fiftieth time, I don't know.'

'It's very important I get there, Olaf.'

'I'm doing my best.'

Loki chuckled to himself.

'I'll bet old Kveld-Ulf's hopping mad.'

'I imagine he is. Now can you shut up, I'm trying to row. Unless you can magic me a wind to blow us the right way. Or maybe you'd like to take a turn with the oars.'

'I have a bad back.'

There was no arguing with it. Loki certainly had every excuse for taking it easy. But that didn't make the blisters on Olaf's hands any less painful. His palms were rubbed sore with handling salty rigging and from pulling at the oars when the wind dropped. On top of that, he was aching with tiredness, having steered the ship all through the night, keeping the boat on track as best he could by using the stars as a guide. At this time of year, he was pretty sure that the seven stars that made Rognir's Wagon should be in the north, while the twin pin-pricks of Thiassi's bright eyes were in the south-east. All through the night he had sailed, and rowed, with only the star-light and the dim luminescence of the wave-riven sea to help him to find the ropes and the oars when they were needed. Dawn was a pink blessing— bringing not only warmth and light, but a reassurance that he was going in roughly the right direction, since the glow of the rising sun could only come from the east. And so he sailed on through the brightening day. By mid-morning, Loki's skin had lost some of its palor, as he recovered from the ordeal of the night before. That was when he started to feel sick.

'Not seasick are you?' asked Olaf.

Loki shook his head. It was an unwise thing to do, because the head-shake was enough to disturb the fragile equilibrium of his stomach. He lunged to the side of the boat, and vomited. Olaf watched with amusement.

'A good tip, when you're going to be sick,' chuckled Olaf, 'is to see which way the wind's blowing first.'

Loki looked down. The dark green of his jerkin was stained with light green vomit, blown back at him by a fierce breeze.

'Thanks,' he growled, before subsiding back into the bottom of the boat.

Just when Olaf was beginning to think that they might actually have evaded Kveld-Ulf, he spotted something. It was only a red dot on the horizon at first, but then it resolved itself into a little square, the shape of a Viking sail. A little while longer, and it was definitely a broad-beamed boat. In fact, a knar. It could only be Kveld-Ulf. Olaf knew that with an expert crew and a good spread of sail, the *Skuldelev* would soon catch up with them. He pulled frantically at the oars, and Loki, realizing that there was something wrong, looked round.

'Is that . . . ?' he enquired.

'I'm afraid so,' squeaked Olaf.

'Oh Hel!' groaned Loki.

And so they continued, with the knarr drawing ever nearer, until Olaf fancied he could pick out a figure standing at the prow and watching the dip and rise of the oars.

'Land!' said Loki, excitedly. 'There.'

Olaf stole a look round, and sure enough, there ahead of them was the broad hump of a small island. Beyond it, another island—this one even smaller.

'Let's go ashore,' Loki squealed.

'Oh yes? And where will we hide, on a little island like that?'

Olaf was right, of course. Landing here would be fatal.

Instead, Olaf steered into the gap between the islands.

'What are you doing?' barked Loki.

'It's going to be shallow between the two islands. If they try and follow us it could rip the bottom out of the *Skuldelev*.'

'Good plan.'

'On the other hand, if it's really shallow, it could easily rip the bottom out of this little boat.'

'And what do we do then?'

'Well, drowning is the usual procedure.'

'Great.'

'Closely followed by death.'

'Thanks.'

From that point, Loki became nervously alert, pointing out every swirl and eddy in the water that might indicate a hidden rock, until Olaf was forced to threaten him that if he didn't shut up, then the axe would go into his back again—and this time would stay there. When they finally emerged from the strait between the two islands, the *Skuldelev* was nowhere in sight.

'Looks like we've lost them—for now,' Olaf breathed.

'I wonder how Kveld-Ulf knew we'd be heading for Norway,' Loki mused. 'Anyway, move over, I'll help with the oar.'

Loki did so. It seemed he was now fully recovered from Kveld-Ulf's murderous attack. With two of them rowing with all their strength, they made a little more headway.

'More land,' said Loki, suddenly, glancing over his shoulder. 'Let's duck into a fjord and hide.'

Olaf didn't say anything, but trimmed the sail and swung the boat around close to the wind. They didn't need to row now. The sail took them scudding in towards the main land-mass ahead.

'Funny kind of fjord,' Loki said. 'More of a curved bay with a load of sandy-coloured cliffs.'

'Yes, strange, isn't it?'

'In fact, if I didn't know better, I'd say it didn't look like Norway at all . . . '

CHAPTER SEVEN

As they approached the shoreline, which was sheltered by projecting headlands, the wind dropped
again, and they took to the oars once more.

'Could you row a bit harder?' Olaf said. 'Come
on, put your back into it.'

'This isn't Norway, is it?' said Loki.

'Look, we're veering off to one side. Faster,
Loki.'

'You lied to me,' said Loki.

'Did I ever say we were going to Norway?'
protested Olaf. 'I told you I was going to find my
father in Angle-land. And that's where we are.
Didn't you notice we were going south rather
than north?'

'I wasn't in any condition to notice where we
were going,' Loki complained, 'I was recovering
from a major axe-wound. And as soon as I got over
that you made sure I was sick.'

'I made you sick?'

'Yes. You kept making the horizon go up and

69

down, and sending the boat through big waves. You tricked me. In fact, I don't think I'll ever be able to . . . '

'Look!' bleated Olaf, pointing along the bay.

The *Skuldelev* was bearing down on them. It had appeared suddenly from behind one of the headlands, and was so close that Kveld-Ulf was clearly recognizable at the prow, bellowing triumphantly.

Loki and Olaf pulled desperately at the oars. They were almost within range of a flung spear, but the *Skuldelev*'s crew were not going to risk losing any more weapons, since it was obvious that they would soon catch them up. There was an occasional scrape along the bottom of the boat, as it began to skim through the shallows. Behind them, the cursing and threats of the crew were loud and frightening.

'Keep rowing,' Olaf shouted. He knew that at least they would be able to get closer to the shore than the bigger vessel. That might make a crucial difference. When the boat finally beached on the sand, Olaf abandoned his oar and leapt into the water. Loki grabbed the hammer and followed. Both blindly flailed through the sea-spray towards the beach. Glancing over his shoulder, Olaf could see that the crew of the *Skuldelev* were leaping over the top-strakes to pull the clumsy ship up onto to the beach.

Olaf and Loki ran on, blindly. A long way ahead, there were some huts, but to one side was a patch of scrubby woodland. It was their one chance of sheltering when the inevitable volley of spears and axes started to rain down. Loki ran remarkably fast for someone recovering from an axe in the back. And fear lent an amazing swiftness to Olaf's legs. They had almost reached the trees before the crew were even halfway up the beach. Then Olaf felt a sharp pain in his head, and found himself collapsing onto the ground.

Olaf opened his eyes, but at first it was difficult to focus on anything. A large nearby blob resolved itself into a figure with a drawn sword—presumably a guard who was there to stop them escaping. A smaller blob became Loki, sitting disconsolately on the ground. When Olaf looked towards the beach, he could see that a battle was in progress. Kveld-Ulf's men were advancing towards the defenders, who had formed a line along the beach in order to prevent the Vikings from reaching their cluster of huts. The Angles were fighting well. Kveld-Ulf's men were having a hard time of it. The crew of the *Skuldelev* were advancing up the beach, but only slowly. And in the middle of the melee, a powerful young Angle with a mop of blond hair was giving them a good deal of trouble, laying about the attackers with a bright battle-hammer that shone emerald and crimson in the sun.

Olaf looked over at Loki, who was watching the fight anxiously, following the precious hammer with his eyes.

'They've stolen it,' he murmured. 'The dung-eating, slime-sucking, scum-gargling, excrescences from a pig's bottom have stolen it.'

'But, Loki, you only had it because you stole it from Kveld-Ulf!' Olaf said. And even though he spoke quietly, so as not to antagonize their guard, every word produced a little bolt of pain in his temples. Olaf touched the top of his head, carefully. As far as he could tell, his brains were still on the inside of his skull, which was a good sign, though his head throbbed from the blow that had knocked him unconscious.

'Yes,' Loki protested, 'but Kveld-Ulf only had it because he stole it from me. At least when I stole it in the first place, I stole it honestly.'

'And who did you steal it from in the first place?' Olaf asked, but Loki clamped his lips shut and carried on watching the glinting hammer.

Now that he could focus his eyes properly, Olaf noticed a column of smoke rising from a bald cliff-top at one end of the bay. He wondered, idly, why anyone would take the trouble to light a fire in such a place on a warm day. Strange people, these Angles. He looked at the guard standing over them, and was surprised to find that he was a gangling, weedy young man, not much older than Olaf himself. And the odd thing about him was that although he evidently belonged to the same tribe as the defenders, he was dressed like . . . well, he was dressed a little like Olaf himself—the tunic and trousers and boots of a Norwegian Viking. His long hair was plaited in the Viking way, and he wore his short sword along his belt—not swinging from it, as the Angles did. Instead of killing them both on the spot, which was what Olaf expected, he crouched down and spoke to them, and in spite of the heavy accent, Olaf could understand pretty well everything he said.

'You real Vikings? You look weird. You like my sword? It's Danish. Good, yeah?'

'How do you know our language?' asked Olaf.

'Language I learn in Jorvic. Do jobs for Viking men there, they give me much coins, give me sword. Run from home, live there, meet many Viking maybe ten, eleven years old, then I come back, I am looking tough Viking, talking tough Viking . . .'

The boy sounded friendly enough, considering he was addressing the deadly enemies of his people. He was gesturing all the time as he spoke, which was difficult as he was holding two swords, one of which was Olaf's.

'Oh, sorry about hit on the head. I have to stop you somehow. I called Brihtric. I much like Viking.'

'You *like* Vikings?' Olaf asked.

'Much like,' he said. 'Like Viking hair-plait, Viking boot, Viking weapon. Many young like me in this country, we like this style. But old people not understand this. That why they don't trust me to fight. They think maybe I turn other side. So they just give me prisoners to guard.'

The boy turned to Loki.

'Him don't look Viking. Look funny little elf-man. Got very hard head though. Six swipes with big stick, he still conscious. Pretty good, I think.'

'Thank you,' Loki said, drily.

'You want I let you go?'

'What?' Olaf could barely believe what he was hearing.

'You take me with. You show me using sword, maybe come Denmark.'

'I don't think that's possible,' Loki said.

'OK,' the boy said, cheerfully. 'In that case, village gets Daneskins.'

'What?'

'Special leather covering. First we take off your skin. If you lucky, we kill you first. Then we nail skin to church door. Nice Daneskin, look good.'

'Tell you what,' said Olaf, 'why don't you come with us?'

'You take me with? You good, real good,' bubbled Brihtric, and handed Olaf his sword. 'You show how make longship, we go Denmark.'

'I'm not going,' Loki pronounced, firmly.

'What?' said Olaf, then wished he hadn't said it quite so loudly and clutched his head.

'I can't leave without the hammer.'

'You stay there then, I'm going.'

'You can't,' snapped Loki.

'Why not?'

'Because I need you to help me to take the hammer back to Norway.'

'Please, we really need go now,' panicked Brihtric. 'They only let you live so they can have fun killing you later.'

'I'm going, Loki. I've helped you as much as I can.'

'Helped me by taking me to Angle-land instead of Norway. Fine. I can do without that kind of help.'

'Well, if that's how you feel, come on, Brihtric, let's go.'

Loki stayed silent, sadly watching the battle. Olaf took a couple of unwilling steps, then turned to Brihtric.

'Do you think if we asked nicely, they'd give him the hammer back?'

Brihtric shook his head. 'If you ask nicely, they use it to smash your skull.'

Olaf knew that he should leave, but he couldn't help feeling concerned for Loki, who surely couldn't go on sustaining fatal injuries without incurring some permanent damage. He stood for a moment, watching the progress of the battle. Kveld-Ulf was confronting the man with the jew-elled war-hammer. With blind ferocity, he aimed a savage axe-swing at his head. The blond man blocked with the hammer, and there was a shower of white-hot sparks as the axe exploded into fragments. The blond man was so taken aback by this turn of events that he stood still for a moment, amazed. It was all the opportunity Kveld-Ulf needed. He lunged head-first at the man's belly, knocking him backwards, then trampled over his prostrate body and snatched the hammer from his grasp. Kveld-Ulf charged on, followed by the rest of the crew. Recovering the hammer had obviously given them new heart, and they easily broke the line of defenders and headed for the huts. They were screaming in triumph now, certain that the small village was at their mercy, and anything of value in the place was theirs for the taking.

As they approached the huts, Kveld-Ulf looked at the little group: Loki sitting resolutely on the ground, Olaf and Brihtric standing nearby. He bellowed in rage, and ran up to Loki, then raised the hammer high above his head. Olaf leapt over to block the blow with his sword. He knew it was futile. The hammer seemed to destroy any weapon it came into contact with, but Olaf couldn't stand by and watch his friend being murdered without putting up some kind of resistance.

Just as Kveld was about to strike, armed men began sprinting along the beach, coming from the headlands at either end of the little bay. In fact, some had already reached the *Skuldelev*, and were dancing around it in triumph. Suddenly, Olaf realized the purpose of the hill-top blaze. It acted as a beacon, to bring reinforcements to fend off Viking raids. And it was certainly working. There seemed to be hundreds of men, as well as a few women, brandishing makeshift weapons and pouring onto the beach from all directions.

Kveld-Ulf paused to take in the situation. His men were clearly out-numbered, and there was no way they would be able to regain the ship. There was now a horde of armed Angles heading for them, baying for blood. Kveld-Ulf clearly had no choice. He made a rapid change of plan, and instead of running towards the village, charged into the woods. For a moment, he brandished the gleaming battle-hammer defiantly, then dived through the undergrowth, accompanied by the rest of his crew.

The Angles ran after them, uttering loud war-whoops. When the last fighting men had disappeared into the foliage, Brihtric turned to the two prisoners.

'Where we go now?' asked Brihtric.

'We'll go north, to find my father,' said Olaf.

'We'll follow Kveld-Ulf and get the hammer back,' said Loki.

'Then this is where we part company,' Olaf said. 'I've sworn to find my father, and that's what I shall do.'

'I can't do it alone,' Loki protested.

'Tough.'

'Olaf,' said Loki, winningly, 'about this hammer . . . '

'Well?' snapped Olaf.

'It's a very special hammer.'

'Yeah, very nice, all the jewels and stuff. But I need to find my father.'

Loki leaned against a tree, and took a deep breath. Olaf sensed that Loki had something important to tell him.

'You see,' Loki continued, 'this isn't *a* hammer. It's *the* hammer. I borrowed it. From a kind of . . . special person. Look, it's a long story, there's no time now.' Olaf nodded. It was important to get away from the village before the warriors returned.

'If to avoid fighting, we go this way, I think,' said Brihtric, softly, and they trudged after him. Ahead, a river snaked on through a little ravine, where they had to walk for a while through the freezing water. Then the river became broad, and shallow, and was crossed by a muddy track through the woods.

'We maybe stop now a while?' Brihtric asked.

Loki and Olaf nodded, and squatted on the ground.

'Did you work out the riddle?' asked Loki.

'Well . . . sort of . . . ' Olaf said. 'Less than a god, more than a man, so you have some kind of supernatural powers . . . '

'That's not quite it, Olaf. You see, I'm not just *called* Loki, I *am* Loki.'

Brihtric broke in.

'So who is this Loki?'

'This is Loki. I mean, Loki is Loki. But what he's trying to make us believe is that he's Loki. I mean, *the* Loki. Which would make him sort of a . . . god. But if you're some kind of god, Loki, then why did you put up with being tied to a post for six months back in our village? Why didn't you just change yourself into a snake, or a bear, or a giant, and escape?'

'It's not that easy,' said Loki.

'So you can't do it?' Olaf said.

'Doing it is fine. It's getting back again that's the problem. I once spent six weeks as a halibut off the coast of Greenland, and I'm not anxious to repeat the experience.'

'How about buckets?' said Olaf.

'Buckets?' said Brihtric, who was now completely bewildered by the whole conversation.

'I wondered if you'd noticed that,' Loki said. 'That was a desperate situation. Didn't you notice that Odin's spies were about?'

'All I saw was a couple of flea-bitten old ravens,' said Olaf.

'Precisely,' said Loki.

'So Loki is . . . who? He is elf-man, bear, bucket, snake, god?' asked Brihtric.

'Well,' Olaf stumbled, ' . . . Loki is . . . Loki is kind of a god. But he likes mischief and tricks. And sometimes the tricks are just harmless, but sometimes they're really vicious. Like when he killed Balder.'

'Who is Balder?' asked Brihtric.

'Balder was a god, and he was really good-looking and clever, and he couldn't be hurt by anyone. But Loki found a way of killing him.'

Brihtric was still not taking it all in.

'This man,' Brihtric said, pointing at Loki, 'this is a god?'

'Yes,' Olaf explained, still trying to come to

terms with the idea himself. 'And he was found wandering around near our village and my uncle took him as a slave and . . . ' Suddenly a thought occurred to Olaf. 'So if you really are *the* Loki, then the hammer . . . '

'Exactly,' said Loki. 'The hammer belongs to Thor, the thunderer of the gods. It can hurl thunderbolts. It can deliver death and destruction a hundred miles away. It can flatten towns and consume forests with fire and tempest.'

'So why did you have it in the first place?'

'I borrowed it.'

'So Thor lent you his precious hammer, and . . . '

'Not exactly. I borrowed it, without actually asking. I was bored; it was an interesting way of passing the time, hurling thunderbolts around the mountains. And I'd just hidden it so I could play with it again the next day . . . '

'So you . . . you . . . stole Thor's hammer . . . '

'Not stole. I borrowed it . . . while Thor was asleep. I was going to sneak it back to his palace. But your idiot villagers captured me before I could do so.'

'What, you mean, you actually . . . you took it and . . . and Thor . . . has been without his hammer for all this . . . '

'Six endless months, while I have been living with barbarians and feeding on scraps. Yes. I imagine he's noticed by now. So you see, recovering the hammer comes before everything. While Thor is without his hammer, he has no defence against the earth-gods and the giants.'

'I see,' said Olaf.

'If they knew he was defenceless, then they would invade Asgard, and Ragnarok would come, and the serpent at the bottom of all things would swallow his own tail, and the world would be consumed in a great pit of fire and destruction.'

'That sound pretty bad,' said Brihtric.

'It's about as bad as can be,' said Loki. 'But even worse, we've got nothing for breakfast in the morning.'

CHAPTER EIGHT

It was hot the next day. The kind of day when you can almost feel the damp weight of the air, pressing down on you. Trees oozed thick gum from their trunks. Loki, Olaf, and Brihtric paused by the side of a green-mantled pool, where frogs floated lazily, eyes just above water.

'Of course, the problem is, we don't really know where they've gone, exactly,' Olaf said.

'Well, maybe,' Brihtric said, 'but many Vikings come round this tree pretty soon ago.'

Olaf and Loki looked at him, blankly.

'See these leaves, crushed into the ground? And here. This is mark of Viking boot. Here someone trip over, see?'

'That's amazing,' said Olaf.

'Nah, just sneaky. We Angles doesn't fight no good, so we learn sneaky tricks like this.'

This was encouraging. Brihtric was turning out to be more useful than they could ever have imagined. He even managed to find food—of a sort—just raw mushrooms, and roots, and green sprouting leaves. It wasn't like having a proper meal though. Olaf's stomach cried out for bread and fish and meat, and his whole body ached for fresh water.

They knew that they would have to keep moving if they were to catch up with the crew of the *Skuldelev*, and so they carried on until the light grew so dim that the trees could barely be seen. Olaf was about to flop down among the bracken, exhausted, when there was a sound—a distant one, but unmistakably the sound of a human voice.

'Is that them?' Olaf asked.

Brihtric nodded. 'There is river—they get there by evening. Good chance they stop there. We follow, yes?'

And they did. Painfully slow it was, in the crushing heat, trudging over the difficult ground. Olaf's legs ached with the effort, but every so often there would be a noise ahead, and he would somehow find the strength to keep going. The sun set, but still they travelled on, through the thickening dusk. And then, at last, the tree-tops were illuminated by a flickering light, and they became aware of the steady growl of conversation.

'They'll have guards,' Loki whispered. 'We need a plan.'

Olaf noticed for the first time that Loki was leaning on a stick—more a small tree-trunk than a stick, really.

'Are you all right?' Olaf asked.

'I'm feeling a bit stiff and groggy,' said Loki. 'Nothing to worry about. Carry on.'

'Right. Well, we'll scout round first. Then we wait until they're asleep, sneak in, and take the hammer,' Olaf murmured.

Brihtric was indignant.

'Sneak? Sneak? This is not Viking way. Viking way is we shout "werrggghhh" . . . '

'Werrrgghhh?' Olaf repeated.

'You know, some loud battle-shout. So, shout "werrrgggghh", or "graggghhh", or "waaarrgghhh", run in fast, kill guards, smash many skulls with axe, then take what we want.'

'It's a great plan,' Olaf said, 'and the only problem I can think of is that it won't work. Mostly because there are thirty-two of them and they're all bigger and stronger than us, oh, and also better armed. Oh, and also better at fighting.'

'So sneaking is the order of the day,' said Loki.

Olaf decided that if they were to stand any chance of escaping with the hammer, they would have to get a good idea of the layout of the place.

Well before they were anywhere near the camp, he led them off the path, and through the undergrowth between the trees.

'What's that?' said a voice from the camp. Olaf recognized it as Harald. Trust Harald to be on his toes when everyone else was half asleep.

'Where?'

'In the trees.'

In response they dropped to their knees. But the voices were approaching, and Olaf could hear the sound of someone slashing at the undergrowth.

'Down!' Olaf hissed, and Brihtric dived, obediently, into the mud. Loki dropped his stick, and crouched.

The voices got closer:

'Could it have been a rabbit or something?'

'Have you ever seen a six foot rabbit with blond hair?'

A nettle was stinging Olaf's cheek, and there was a blade of grass poking into his left nostril, but he clenched his teeth grimly and kept still.

'Forget it, it must have been my imagination,' said Harald, and the footsteps retreated towards the firelight.

When all was quiet again, they began to crawl through the undergrowth, until they could get a look at the layout of the camp. There was a large fire in the middle, and Kveld-Ulf was lying next to it, already asleep. Olaf scanned around in the half-light, and was at last rewarded. There, on the ground near Kveld-Ulf, was the distinctive leather case in which Ulf stored the hammer. There was a guard at either end of the camp. Lief Twisty-Nose, grey-bearded and plump, leaned against a tree with folded arms encircling a spear whose honed barbs glittered in the firelight. The other, whom Olaf recognized as Thorvald Hairy-Breeks, stood alert, with his spear thrust into the ground next to him. But there was no sign of a guard on the path leading away from the river, and that seemed the best way in, since it would take them closer to Kveld-Ulf, and would be quieter than coming in through the dense undergrowth.

'Now we wait for them to sleep,' Olaf hissed.

They crawled away, some distance from the camp, and huddled in the shelter of a tree, Loki leaning heavily on his stick as he crouched down. When there had been no sound from the camp for a good while, Olaf cautiously crawled through the undergrowth to see what was going on. By now, the Vikings were all lying flat out, eyes closed. Except the guards, of course.

'They're asleep,' Olaf whispered, when he had made his way back to Loki and Brihtric.

'I go first,' Brihtric said.

'Yes, but Loki's lightest on his feet,' Olaf said. 'Like a cat, aren't you, Loki?'

'Well,' Loki said, 'I'd be happy to go but . . . '

Grasping his stout stick, he made an attempt to get up, but then groaned, and sank to the ground.

'What's wrong?' said Olaf.

'So sorry,' whimpered Loki, 'I don't think I can do it. Must be the axe-wound.'

'You get hit with axe and still alive?' said Brihtric. 'You real lucky.'

'It didn't feel lucky at the time,' said Loki. Then he gave a little grunt, and clutched his shoulder.

'Are you going to be all right?' Olaf asked.

'I'll be fine,' croaked Loki. 'Just need some time to recover. It's been agony for a while, but I didn't like to say anything.'

'Don't you worry, Loki,' said Olaf. 'We'll get the hammer, and then come back for you.'

'Thank you,' said Loki, with a brave smile, and he settled back against a tree-trunk and pulled his cloak around his shoulders.

Slowly, cautiously, Brihtric and Olaf made their way towards the camp.

'I wonder why they didn't put a guard on this path?' Olaf murmured.

'Who cares?' whispered Brihtric. 'Now if I may just take a quick leak. I sneak much better on an empty bladder.'

'All right. Hurry.'

Brihtric leaned against a tree to relieve himself.

There was a gentle sound of splashing liquid, followed by an almighty roaring sound from nearby. Olaf's mind ran through the range of possibilities. A bear? A wolf? Or . . . or . . . And this was the strongest possibility, maybe there *had* been a guard at this end of the clearing. A guard who had gone to sleep behind a tree. A guard who just happened to be in the line of fire when Brihtric relieved himself.

It was Brihtric who was the first to work out what was going on. He pulled up his leggings, drew his sword, and said:

'Looks like it's the Viking way after all.' And he followed this with a fierce battle cry. It could have been 'werrggghhh', or 'wargghhh', Olaf didn't know, because action had suddenly become urgent. At full speed, he charged into the clearing, uttering his own war-cry at the top of his voice.

Olaf made for Kveld-Ulf. The leather bag was still

there, lying on the ground next to him. Kveld had never been quick to wake up, and was still lying down. Olaf snatched the leather bag, and sprinted back the way he had come. At once, six figures converged on him, gripping the precious bag hard. Olaf clung on, tenaciously, but he knew he couldn't hold on for long. Brihtric began flailing at the Vikings with his sword, and several of them had to let go of the bag in order to defend themselves. The last to let go was Harald, strongest of the party, who hung on as determinedly as Olaf himself. That was when Olaf's eyes became clouded and the struggling figures and the flickering fire began to burn red. He knew now that the strength of the berserker was descending on him. With a mighty heave, he retrieved the bag, and when Harald slashed at him with his sword, he was ready to block, and to counter-attack ferociously. Harald only survived by a frenzy of blocking and side-stepping. Then Brihtric and Olaf were shoulder to shoulder, both belabouring their attackers, blow after blow.

'Run,' Brihtric said. 'You have what you want.'

It took a moment for Brihtric's words to get through. Olaf had been so incensed that he hardly remembered what he had come for. More Vikings were joining the attack now. They couldn't hold them off for ever. He delivered a final blow at Harald's helmet, which rang out in the night air, and then he turned and fled, closely followed by Brihtric.

Kveld-Ulf barked out a rage-strangled cry of 'Get them!' but soon they were lost in the darkness, heading back for the place where they had left Loki. That was when Olaf became uneasy. The bag seemed remarkably light. Olaf had never actually held the hammer himself, but from its appearance, it should have been a fairly hefty weight. He patted the bag with his hand.

'Brihtric, we have to go back.'

'Back?'

'The hammer. It's not here. The bag is empty.'

'Bag may be empty, but my head not. I not going back.'

'But we have to, you see . . . where's Loki?'

'He gone.'

'But he wouldn't go. Why would he go? He wasn't well.'

Olaf screamed, 'Loki!' The cry reverberated around the forest. Brihtric shushed him desperately, dragging him away by the elbow.

'We must go. Must.'

'But we can't. Maybe they've got him already.'

'Maybe. But must to go now. Very now.'

Olaf knew he was right. The sounds of bootsteps were getting closer. And off they ran, at a desperate pace, into the depths of the forest.

And so the night went on. They collided with trees that were invisible in the moonless blackness. They came across the stream again, and Olaf wondered for an awful moment if they had doubled back to the Viking camp. They froze in terror when they spotted a menacing-looking figure that turned out to be a small tree, and then strolled casually past a tree that turned out to be a large Viking. They crouched in a patch of nettles for a while, before once again hearing the sounds of pursuit. Lungs strained for breath. Legs ached. Hearts thumped with the continual effort. After an eternity of hiding and crawling and running, a little light began to filter through the trees. On they ran. A little way ahead, the trees stopped, on the edge of open country. They staggered on, exhausted. Then an armed figure dropped from a tree, straight in front. There was no time to react. Olaf could only hope he would be killed quickly. Maybe when he was dead, he might be allowed to rest a little. But as it turned out, it was not an axe-wielding Viking, but Loki. In his hand was the shining, jewelled hammer.

'What kept you?' grinned Loki.

Olaf and Brihtric were speechless.

'I just had this feeling that sneaking wasn't going to work,' Loki explained. 'Or shouting "werrrggghhh", come to that. But I thought you might cause a useful diversion. And you did.'

'What?'

'Well, did you really think Kveld would leave the hammer in its case ready to be snatched? He always slept with it clutched to his chest. But once he'd sent everyone off to chase after you two, it was easy to creep up on him and slug him from behind with a handy tree-trunk, I mean, walking-stick.'

'Loki not ill, he just pretend!' said Brihtric, still trying to work it out.

'I can't believe it,' snarled Olaf. 'And we were worried about you. You slimy, sneaky, lying . . .'

'Thanks for all the complimentary words, but I think we should keep going. Don't you?'

Their pursuers were not far behind. And so they left the cover of the trees, and ran on, over the sparse, brown turf, heading up a steep hill. But the sounds of pursuit grew relentlessly closer. Halfway up the incline was a little patch of spiky gorse. Brihtric flung himself into it, and Loki and Olaf followed. The prickles scratched at hands and faces, and thrust themselves uncomfortably through woollen stockings, but they kept still and quiet for a moment, looking back towards the woods for signs of life.

Very soon, four of Kveld's crew emerged from the wood. Kveld-Ulf himself was among them. He started to take his men uphill, but then shook his head and led his companions back towards the forest. Then he gestured them to stop, and bent down to look at something on the ground. He stood, grinning, and began once more to head in their direction, following the tracks in the flattened grass. Olaf bowed his head, and curled up as small as the prickling twigs and thorns would allow.

Then there was a voice, very close by. It was Egil.

'In the gorse-bushes. Come on. Flush them out!'

With glee, the Vikings started to poke at the bushes with spears and swords. The three fugitives dodged and ducked, insofar as it is possible to dodge and duck while curled up in a gorse-bush. Olaf pleaded:

'Loki, do something!'

That was when Olaf heard the noise. There was a fierce sound, and the smack of sword on shield, as if a party of men were charging down the hillside towards them. Kveld-Ulf, who had raised his sword to swipe at Brihtric, turned on his heel and fled. And small wonder. There was a thump of angry bootsteps approaching, and fierce cries.

'Well done, Loki, that was amazing!' said Olaf, emerging from the torturing gorse.

'But, Olaf, I didn't do anything,' said Loki.

'Yes you did. You made a sound like a group of heavily armed Angle warriors.'

That was when Olaf looked around and realized that they were surrounded by a group of heavily armed Angle warriors.

CHAPTER NINE

Garram looked Thor over, from top to toe.

'Your cloak-pin's upside-down, there's gravy on your tunic, your belt's crooked, your boots need a clean, and there's a big hole in your socks. But actually, that's quite good for you. Come on.'

Thor straightened his belt, ran his fingers through his tousled hair, and started to sway down the corridor towards the sacred part of the palace where Odin lived. A white-bearded servant stood at the door of Odin's hall. Garram opened his mouth to ask for permission to enter, but the guard simply put a finger to his lips, and gestured them to stop. They did so.

A long time went by. Then nothing happened. After that a good deal more time went by. Then for no particular reason, the guard stepped aside and slowly swung open the door. The only lighting in the huge hall was a single flaming torch. From the doorway, it seemed as distant as the pole star on a sharp winter night. Garram and Thor began to step towards it, slowly. As they got closer, Odin could be seen, in the light of the burning torch, hunched over a piece of parchment on which many runes were inscribed. Hugin and Munin were perched, motionless, on his shoulders. With hesitant steps, Thor and Garram approached, and when they had reached a point which was close enough for conversation but distant enough to be respectful, they knelt, heads down. Thor addressed Odin:

'O Odin, god of war and wisdom, of poetry and death, Odin all-father, also called Alfdaur, Bileygr, Ouvin, Glapsudir, Othinn, Woden, Wode, and Wotan . . . '

Odin looked up, and stared at them a moment with his one eye. The eyelid over the other, empty, eye-socket twitched briefly.

'Sorry, I was miles away,' he said. 'What were you saying?'

Thor cleared his throat and began again:

'O Odin, god of war and wisdom, of poetry and death, Odin all-father, also called Alfdaur . . . '

'Yes yes,' interrupted Odin, impatiently, the eyelid over the empty eye-socket twitching once more. 'What did you actually want?'

'It's about the hammer.'

'Oh, is that all,' said Odin, glancing down at the runes again.

'It's quite important, actually, O Odin, god of war and of poetry . . . '

'Well, as it happens, I already know about the missing hammer, so if you'll just let me get on . . . '

'Odin, without the hammer, the Giants can roam free. That means Ragnarok. Death, destruction, ruin, and blood. The end of the world.'

'Yes yes, I know. It's all at hand.'

There was silence for a moment. Odin consulted the runes again, then looked up.

'Sorry, did I say it was all at hand? I meant, it's all *in* hand. I've known about the problem for some time.'

'Oh? How long, Odin all-father?'

'About three thousand years.'

'Three thousand years? But Odin, it only went missing six months ago.'

'Yes, well, I don't like having to deal with things at the last minute. It is all in hand. The hammer is on its way back.'

'On its way back?' asked Thor. 'So . . . when do I get it?'

Odin looked at his runes again.

'Ah. Now when I said it was on its way back, I

didn't actually say it was going to *get* here.'

'Oh,' groaned Thor, disappointed. 'Will it get here?'

Another pause. Odin rested a slender finger on one of the runes for a moment, thinking.

'I don't know,' Odin said. 'It could be that tomorrow will bring Ragnarok, death, destruction, ruin. On the other hand . . . '

'Yes?' twittered Garram, unable to get through another long pause.

'On the other hand, it could be scattered showers and sunny spells, with a slight ground-frost overnight.'

'But, Odin, all-father, will he get the . . . ' gibbered Garram.

A deep voice spoke behind them.

'It is over.'

Garram twittered. Thor groaned. The guardian of Odin's door had followed them the length of the hall without either of them realizing it. Odin was lost in his runes again now, with Hugin and Munin happily settled on his shoulders . . .

'Anything you'd like me to remember?' asked Munin.

'Anything you want thought about?' said Hugin.

But Odin sat there, motionless in the half-light,

his one eye fixed on the runes, as Thor and Garram followed the door-guardian back out of the hall.

They were back at the village, with its long view down the beach to the sea, where the *Skuldelev* still lay at the water's edge. The village consisted of a circle of thatched huts, with a space in the middle where a large fire was burning. Around the fire was a group of Angles, who were busy sharpening an assortment of spears. Olaf looked across at Loki.

'What do you think they're going to do with us?' Olaf asked.

'Well, it's just a wild guess, but I have this strange feeling they're going to do their best to . . . kill us.'

Brihtric tried to smile winningly at their captors, and then had a brief conversation with them in his own language.

'What did he say?' Olaf asked. 'Are they going to kill us now?'

'He say no,' Brihtric translated.

'Phew!'

'No, he says they're going to have a big party.

103

Their chief is going to come. *Then* they're going to kill us.'

After some time, a small, scruffy man with a ragged cloak roughly tied at the throat arrived. He jabbered something to the people round the fire. They seemed to get excited about this.

'He say their chief is coming now, so get the spears ready,' Brihtric translated.

Minutes went by, and the men kept looking expectantly in the direction of the woods. Then he arrived. A fierce-looking man, big-bearded, and with eyes that shone blue in the firelight. He took a skin and drank deeply from it, and sat by the fire. He jabbered at them, and in response they smiled, and laughed. Then someone pointed to the prisoners. The chief looked at them for the first time, and then spoke to the Angles. Six of them dragged the helpless prisoners up to the firelight. The chief's blue eyes shone with contempt. Two of the Angles went to get the spears from where they were leaning, against the nearest house. Olaf and Loki were held, arms outstretched, as the two Angles with the spears prepared to take a run at them.

Then the chief turned to Olaf and said:

'Anything you want to say before you die?'

It took a moment for Olaf to work out why it was that he could understand what was being said. Then he realized that the man was speaking in Norse.

'Yes,' Olaf said.

'Well, go on, we haven't got all night.'

'Hello, father.'

CHAPTER TEN

They were sitting at the fireside, chewing meat and washing it down with ale. Olaf's father didn't look quite so frightening now. Olaf had been given back his sword, which was thrust into his belt. Brihtric had gone a little way off to chat with some Angle boys of his own age, and was proudly showing them his Viking sword. Loki sat next to Olaf, with the hammer cradled in his lap, picking delicately at the meat from a sheep-bone.

It seemed Olaf's father had done the usual mix of raiding and trading for the first six months he'd been away and had done well. They had stolen golden chalices and plate from a monastery in Ireland, and many gold coins from settlements along the coast of Angle-land, and were returning for the home trip when a storm had forced them to turn back. But they hadn't got back to Angle-land in time to avoid being shipwrecked. Sigurd stumbled ashore, not far from this very place, and the local people, instead of putting him to death in some horrible way (which was what he had expected) had looked after him until he recovered from his ordeal. His first plan had been to wait for a Viking raiding party to strike somewhere near, and get a ride home with them, but before he had a chance to do so, he had learned the Angles' language and their ways, and by the time a raiding party came to terrorize the coastline, he actually helped the locals to fight against them, winning a famous victory. From that point, they had all regarded him as their leader.

'Shame,' Olaf said. 'All that gold and silver, lost at the bottom of the sea.'

'Yes,' Sigurd said, looking away. 'Lucky for me the locals were friendly. They helped me. And I was able to help them. In many different ways.'

'When you say "help", you mean you taught them to fight against your own people?' Olaf interjected.

'If you want to put it like that. It just seems a little more fair that way really. If you're going to have a fight, well . . . ' He paused a moment, sensing Olaf's disapproval. 'Remember the horse-fights, back home?'

'What about them?'

'Would you set a strong stallion against a foal?'

108

'Well, of course not. It wouldn't be any fun.'

'You see? I'm just making things even.'

'It's an interesting point,' Loki said, throwing his meat-bone into the fire. 'No warrior goes to the Valholl without fighting bravely, and you can't fight bravely against people who can't fight back.'

'Exactly. You see, Olaf, by training these people to fight, I'm helping our own people as much as I'm helping them.'

Olaf wasn't convinced, but decided to let it go at that.

'Anyway,' Sigurd said, 'I'm coming back with you, make no mistake about that. But there are things here that make it a little . . . difficult.'

'The villagers? They'll manage without you,' Olaf protested.

'It's not just them. You see, I don't know how to explain this, Olaf, but you see, there's a woman here . . .'

'Father, there are women back home. And we've got our very own ship to go home in.'

"The *Skuldelev*?' said Sigurd. 'I can't believe you're still sailing that decayed old wash-tub. It was only fit for firewood when I left home in the *Freja*. Has Kveld-Ulf done nothing while I've been away?'

'He's drunk a fair bit of ale, and broken wind a lot,' Loki put in.

Sigurd nodded. 'Sounds like my dear brother Kveld-Ulf.'

'So you're coming home with us?' said Olaf, anxiously.

'It's really very important that I get back to Norway,' Loki urged.

'Well, maybe. The big problem is the crew . . .'

'Well, there's me, and Loki,' Olaf said, 'and Brihtric would probably come over . . .'

'Don't count on me for great seamanship,' Loki said, 'but I'm sure we'll be fine. No problem. And there must be some of these villagers who'd make the trip, wouldn't they?'

'You think so?' said Sigurd. 'That would be a little like inviting a bunch of mice to pay a visit to a colony of cats.'

'Please, father? It's really important that Loki gets back.'

'We'll see. If we can get some supplies together and find some volunteers to come with us. But now, let's sleep.'

He jabbered at one of the Angles, who showed Olaf and Brihtric and Loki to bed-spaces in one of the huts, where they collapsed onto heaps of blankets.

Propping himself up on one arm, Olaf noticed that Loki had taken the war-hammer to bed with him. He was evidently anxious not to lose it again. Loki lay on his back, eyes closed. In the light of the fire that came in through the open doorway there was a glitter of jewels. There were runes engraved on the handle which seemed to glow in the half-light. Olaf reached out to touch the first rune, a beautifully inscribed thorn.

'Don't touch that!' Loki snapped.

'Is that what makes it hurl thunderbolts?'

Loki didn't answer, but tucked it out of sight, under his pile of blankets.

Incredibly, Sigurd managed to find several Angles willing to help crew the *Skuldelev* back to Norway. And so they spent the next morning packing the old knarr with food and fresh water. There was a final, hasty meal of roasted meat and flat bread, after which Sigurd packed his few belongings and began to say his goodbyes to the villagers. Then he came to speak to Olaf.

'I need someone to help me,' he said, 'someone I can trust.'

Without another word, he led Olaf towards the

woods. At the last house in the village, he picked up a shovel that was leaning against a shed.

'Where are we going?' asked Olaf.

'You'll see.'

Sigurd selected a spot overgrown with fern and tangled brambles, and began hacking at the under-growth with the spade. Eventually he had scraped a rough circle of soft earth. After a little digging, the spade hit something. A hollow, wooden some-thing. Working with his hands now, Sigurd pushed aside the damp soil until the lid of a battered sea-chest was revealed. Sigurd gestured to one of the handles, and Olaf lifted. They placed the box next to the hole, and Sigurd pulled open the lid. There was a heavy creak as the rusted hinges yielded.

Inside the box was a huge hoard of silver coins, stamped with foreign writing and embossed with the heads of eastern potentates. Olaf was speech-less for a moment.

Then he said, 'Achggghhhhwoooo!'

It was the most coherent speech he could man-age, in the circumstances.

'We managed to recover some of the loot from the *Freja*, you see, me and the Angle villagers. That was one of the reasons why I wasn't flayed and fried when I first got here. Nothing like a little

112

treasure to oil the wheels of diplomacy. But this one I kept for myself.'

By the time they had heaved the chest into the *Skuldelev*, the children had gathered to wave them off. Sigurd picked up one of the little boys and spoke gently to him, before setting him down on the ground.

Brihtric was in an agony of indecision about what to do next.

'You think I should come Denmark with you? Or stay in village? Hm?'

'It's Norway, not Denmark, and it's up to you, if you want to come to Skirringsvijk with us. But maybe you're better off with your own people.'

'But it's so boring with my own people,' said Brihtric, and he bit his lip in concentration for a moment, trying to come to a decision.

'No,' he said, finally, 'I am Viking. I choose Viking weapon, Viking language. I come with you.'

When they had loaded their possessions on board, they began to shoulder the old *Skuldelev* into the water. That was when the villagers began screaming and pointing. Olaf looked up, and round the corner of the headland, a group of armed men was running. At their head, a large, grey-bearded Viking.

It was Kveld-Ulf.

'Go,' said Loki, clutching his precious hammer.

Olaf looked along the beach at the advancing Vikings, uncertain what to do.

'It's the boat they want. Just go,' screamed Loki.

'But if they can't get the boat, then they'll attack somewhere else . . . '

Loki shrugged, and dropped the hammer into the *Skuldelev*, then scrambled over the top-strake into the boat.

'Olaf, get some of these oafs to push us out to sea. We have to get this thing back to Norway.'

Olaf ignored him, and looked up the beach towards the village. Already, the children were being hurried back towards the huts.

'Loki, we need everyone we can get,' pleaded Olaf. 'Come on, fight!'

But Loki had ducked out of sight now, and was silent.

The only people with weapons available were those who had been about to put to sea, and Sigurd gestured and screamed at them, until they were standing in line, between the attackers and the boat. The other villagers were all flooding back to the huts—some of them, Olaf hoped, to collect weapons. Olaf drew his sword.

He spotted a gap in the line of defenders, and ran to it. Soon the enemy was upon them. He laid blow after blow on the shield of his opponent. Then the villager on Olaf's left managed a lucky jab with his spear, which must have pierced the arm of the shield-bearer, because the shield crashed to the ground, leaving the man clutching at a bloodied gash to his wrist. For a moment, Olaf stared helplessly at the man, who was now raising a hand-axe to strike him. Olaf had his sword ready for a two-handed forward thrust that would have gone deep into his chest. But before striking, Olaf looked at the man's face. It was Harald. Both stood motionless for a moment, before Harald swiped his axe at Olaf's sword, sending it spinning away to his left. Harald pulled back the axe to aim a blow at Olaf's unprotected head. The defenceless boy could only stand and wait for the inevitable end.

But before Harald could strike, Olaf caught sight of something flying through the air towards him from the direction of the boat. He caught it squarely in both hands, and used it to block the fearsome blow of Harald's axe, which shattered into a thousand shards as it made contact with the bejewelled weapon. Now it was Harald's turn to stand defenceless, waiting for the fatal blow. But by now some of the villagers had returned, with their weapons, and the line of Kveld-Ulf's force retreated. The startled Harald backed off with them. The villagers rallied round the fearsome figure of Sigurd, and Kveld-Ulf's men fell back some distance from him, warily holding their weapons ready to defend themselves.

Olaf ran to Sigurd's side. The hammer was now his only weapon, and he used it to jab and block as the group around Sigurd continued their attack. It seemed nothing could stand in their way, until they were confronted by the largest and ugliest of the enemy.

Kveld-Ulf was bellowing incoherently as he strode towards them, axe in one hand, sword in the other, flailing mercilessly. Soon he and Sigurd were within a sword's length of each other. Kveld-Ulf swung with his sword, but Sigurd swiped at it furiously, and the sword flew out of Kveld-Ulf's hand. At that moment, Olaf saw that Egil had somehow positioned himself so that he could attack Sigurd from behind. It was a huge effort, but Olaf managed to raise the hammer high enough to block the blow, and Egil's sword disintegrated in a shower of sparks. Now Kveld-Ulf attacked with his hand-axe, but Sigurd was ready, blocking the blow with his own axe. And that was when Sigurd and Kveld-Ulf recognized each other.

Kveld-Ulf was amazed to recognize Sigurd. Sigurd was amazed to recognize Kveld-Ulf, and Olaf was amazed that Kveld-Ulf and Sigurd hadn't recognized each other before. Sigurd was the first to recover his wits. He sprang forward, bringing down the handle of his axe on Kveld-Ulf's arm. Kveld-Ulf's weapon fell to the ground. In a moment, Sigurd was holding the keen edge of his axe against Kveld-Ulf's throat.

Kveld-Ulf pleaded.

'How about we fight, properly, uh? Like in the old days,' Kveld-Ulf wheedled. 'Remember when we were kids?'

'Of course. You used to beat me senseless with a tree-trunk.'

'Exactly,' said Kveld-Ulf. 'Good times, Sigurd. Great times. Remember how you used to whack me across the back of the neck with that wooden club?'

Sigurd's face softened for a moment. He smiled, fondly.

'I did, didn't I?'

'You were pretty good with that club,' Kveld-Ulf said, warmly.

'You were pretty good with that tree-trunk.'

'You remember,' Kveld-Ulf chuckled, 'how you got me on the forehead at sixty paces with that slingshot? I've still got the scar!'

'So you have!' said Sigurd, excitedly. 'And I've still got a mark where you hit me with a spear.'

'So, what do you say?' said Kveld-Ulf. 'Brothers?'

'Brothers,' said Sigurd, clapping him on the shoulder. 'But we still fight, of course.'

'Exactly,' said Kveld-Ulf. 'We should settle this man to man.'

The fight was as furious as only a fight between brothers can be. They swung the heavy swords at each other, until both were sweating and red-faced. Sigurd's sword-blade broke under a merciless swipe aimed at his head, but he fought on with the broken blade, until, swords locked, it became a simple trial of strength as each tried to edge his blade towards his brother's throat. Though Kveld-Ulf was bigger, he was panting harder. Slowly, Sigurd bore down on him, until the blade was actually touching Kveld-Ulf's neck. Kveld-Ulf smiled.

'You win,' he said. 'Well fought, brother.' Sigurd took Kveld-Ulf's sword from his hand and thrust it into the dirt, then turned his back to acknowledge the cheers of the villagers. That was when Kveld-Ulf threw the dagger. Olaf watched helplessly as he pulled it from his belt, and without getting up from the ground, sent it spinning into Sigurd's left shoulder. Sigurd collapsed forwards on the ground, with the dagger still sticking out of his shoulder-blade. Kveld-Ulf rose, unsteadily, then pulled his sword out of the earth. He raised it high above his head, and was about to bring it down onto his brother's skull, when there was a blinding flash of light. The sword in Kveld's raised hands glowed red, then white, then shattered. And as he lay there, stunned and blinded by the lightning-bolt, Sigurd summoned the last of his strength to draw the dagger from his own belt, and send it spinning into Kveld-Ulf's heart. Ulf's legs buckled under him, and he collapsed onto the ground, stone dead.

All eyes turned to Olaf, who held the jewelled hammer limply, until Loki took it from him.

'Well, you've really done it now,' Loki murmured. 'That'll tell every giant from Scandinavia to Vinland that Thor has lost his hammer.'

Sigurd was still conscious, though bleeding heavily, when Olaf reached him.

'What a piece of luck,' he gasped. 'A thunderbolt at exactly the right moment.'

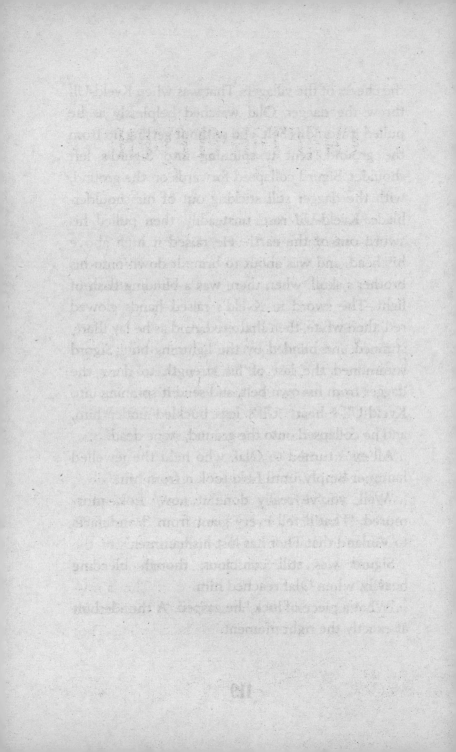

CHAPTER ELEVEN

'He's back then,' said Hugin.

'How can you tell?' Garram said.

'By a sequence of highly intelligent inferences, strung together into the only cohesive explanation for certain phenomena.'

'Phenomawhat?' asked Garram.

'Don't interrupt him,' said Munin. 'He'll forget where he is and then he'll have to start again.'

'As I was saying,' snapped Hugin, 'as I was . . . actually, what was I saying?'

'The only cohesive explanation for certain phenomena,' prompted Munin.

'Ah, exactly. For example, I observe the door, hanging off its hinges and drastically in need of repair. I observe a boot-print on your face, Garram, no doubt caused by the impact of the said boot when thrown at you in response to some tactless enquiry about the success of Thor's mission. I observe a Thor-shaped hole in the door to Thor's room, occasioned, I deduce, when Thor decided to enter it but could not be bothered to open the door. But most of all, I observe Thor himself, hunched in a gibbering heap in the corner of said room. From which I further deduce that Thor's plan was not entirely successful.'

'Well, I tried to tell him,' said Garram. 'But he said he could deal with the threat from the giants with or without his precious hammer.'

'Oh, dear,' said Hugin.

'Oh, bum,' said Munin.

'So off he goes to Jottenheim, armed only with a toasting fork and a dustbin lid, and challenges all the giants to mortal combat.'

'Oh, dear,' said Hugin.

'Six at a time.'

'Oh, bum,' said Munin.

'Apparently, it took him four hours to get his ankles back into the right position.'

'What, had he sprained them?' asked Hugin.

'No, they were wrapped around his neck. Similarly, his arms were plaited around his legs. A bit like a bird, trussed up and ready for the oven.'

'Ouch,' said Hugin.

'Wash your mouth with soap and water!' said Munin.

'So, there it is. Thor can't defeat the giants by

force. Our only hope is that a plan can be devised that is of such fiendish cleverness and complexity that it would tax every sinew of the most powerful intellect in the world. We are all going to depend on the power of Thor's brain.'

'Oh, dear,' said Hugin.

'Oh, bum,' said Munin.

Harald and the surviving crew were remarkably patient about staying in the place so long after the battle. True, there had been the burials of Kveld-Ulf and their other former comrades to deal with, but they didn't seem in any hurry to go home. Loki was furious about this. He had persuaded the crew to take him back with them, and he became daily more anxious. He was all for starting back straight away, and returning later to collect Sigurd. But the crew waited on, resolutely. It all became clear when Harald approached Olaf one morning.

'We're waiting for Sigurd,' he said. 'He is leader, since he defeated Kveld-Ulf.'

'He'll come as soon as he's well enough for the journey,' Olaf said, stiffly.

Harald walked a few steps, then turned, shyly.

'By the way,' he said, 'when I was about to take your head off in the battle . . . '

'Yes?'

'It was nothing personal.' Harald smiled, and walked back to his comrades.

Sigurd remained unconscious for three days, and Olaf was told to expect the worst. He sat by his father's side for hours on end, listening to his laboured breathing. Then Sigurd's eyes opened, and Olaf bent close, to hear his dying whisper:

'Bring me a skinful of mead,' he said.

Olaf didn't think a whole skinful was wise, but he brought a cupful, and held it to his lips. Sigurd drank, greedily. Then he slept again.

Olaf was not used to strong drink, and he woke with a fierce headache, hardly able to remember the events of the night before, when the celebration of Sigurd's victory had taken place. The Angles had postponed the party until Sigurd could stand upright, which was ironic really, because he had spent the evening drinking enough mead to put him flat on his back until well into the next morning. There had been singing, and a good deal of laughing. There had also been dancing, in which Olaf had unwisely participated until he inadvertently danced into a tree. Someone must have put him to bed, because he woke in one of the houses, covered in animal furs. He staggered into the early sunlight, tripping over the bodies of several sleeping villagers as he went. Olaf's father was sleeping where he had fallen the night before, next to the now dying fire. Olaf walked over to him.

'Father, we're going now, and I want you to come with us.'

'Well, Olaf, you see . . . I don't know how to explain this but . . . Well, the truth is . . . You see, what happened was . . .'

And that was when the woman came. She was carrying a wooden bowl of steaming porridge, evidently for Sigurd's breakfast, and a small, fair-haired boy of maybe three or four was trotting along close behind her.

'Well, perhaps it's easier for me to show you than to tell you.' He gestured towards the small boy, who was now running across to jump on his stomach.

'Olaf, meet your little brother, Halfdan.'

Olaf looked at the little boy. By now, Halfdan was sitting on Sigurd's chest, pulling at his hair,

125

and Sigurd laughed at him, affectionately. Olaf's mouth flapped open for a moment.

'Oh, and your stepmother, Wulfruna.'

'You could . . . bring them with us,' Olaf said, uncertainly.

'They don't even speak our language.'

'We could teach them.'

Sigurd hesitated. He looked at the woman.

'No. The boy isn't old enough for a sea-voyage now.'

'So you're leaving me to go back alone.'

'No, I'm coming with you. Brihtric can look after things here. He knows more about Viking combat skills than any Viking I know. I can come back later and collect them.'

'So that's why you were worried about leaving the place.' Olaf felt better about things now. 'You actually do want to come home so that you can spend some time with me.'

'Well, partly. But mostly I want to find out what that scumbucket Grimnir's been doing with my village.'

CHAPTER TWELVE

Olaf stood with Sigurd at the prow of the *Skuldelev*, which was now approaching the sheltered bay near his home village. A few people came out of the houses to watch them coming in. Olaf had no doubt that when they arrived, there would be plenty of feasting and celebration—which would be very welcome after a voyage in which they had eaten only oat-biscuits and dried walrus meat.

It was Grimnir himself who greeted them as they climbed out onto the jetty.

'Oh, you're back then,' he said, unenthusiastically. Then he recognized Sigurd. 'You!' he exclaimed.

'Yes, me, Grimnir. And I hope you and my brother have looked after things properly while I've been away.'

'During the six *years* you've been away.'

'Is it really that long? Well well. And where's the feast?'

Grimnir almost laughed in his face.

'Feast! Hah! You'll be lucky. Nothing to feast *on*. Except oat biscuits and dried walrus meat.'

'Grimnir,' Olaf said, 'would you please get us a drink and tell us what has been going on here?'

'Where is Kveld-Ulf?' Grimnir asked, suspiciously.

'Dead. It's a long story.'

There was a pause.

'Dead, you say.'

'Yes, I'm afraid so,' said Sigurd. 'Now can we come in?'

They were in the longhouse, sitting at a big table. And the older people—those who had been left behind during the voyage—brought ale and oatcakes for the men who had returned. But there was none of the celebration that normally took place after a homecoming. They certainly didn't seem overjoyed to see Sigurd, after his six-year absence. They barely looked up from the table when he came in after having a look around the farm. He approached Grimnir, accusingly.

'Where are they?' Sigurd said, looking Grimnir straight in the eye. Grimnir looked away, and fiddled with a loose thread on his woollen stocking.

'I had to let them go.'

Sigurd grasped the neck of Grimnir's tunic, and pulled him to his feet. Then he hoisted him off the ground and held him, feet dangling in the air, and spat the words at his face:

'What happened to the cattle?'

'You're choking me!' said Grimnir, in panic.

Sigurd composed himself. He lowered Grimnir until his feet rested on the ground, and then straightened the collar of Grimnir's jerkin.

'Let's take this quietly, shall we? Don't worry, I'm not going to hurt you. Just tell the truth, then we'll have a calm, civilized discussion about this. Now what happened to the cattle?'

'Sold them,' said Grimnir. Then he blurted out, 'No point trying to keep them, with giants wandering round all night, stealing them.'

'Giants?' said Sigurd.

'That's right. You wouldn't know, not being here, but there's been giants here just lately.'

'It's true,' said old Mother Thorun. 'Never seen nothing like it in my life. Them giants has been stomping and stamping and stumbling all over the place, gobbling up the cattle.'

'That's right,' Grimnir said, 'giants kept taking the cattle. So I sold 'em.'

'You see?' said Sigurd, quietly. 'That wasn't so hard, was it? Now, where's the money?'

'Gone.'

Sigurd made a visible effort to control himself.

'Gone you say. Right. Where has the money gone?'

'None of your business.'

'What!'

'It's nothing to do with you. You've been away six years. Kveld-Ulf put me in charge until he came back. And he's not back.'

Sigurd's face was purple. His fists were bunched into tight clubs. Once again, Grimnir was hoisted off the floor.

'You snivelling, sneaking goat's-bladder full of mouldering pus, you foul stinking excretion from a disease-infected pig, you dung-covered . . .'

'Father, you have plenty of silver, haven't you . . . ?'

'Well?'

'Well, can't you just . . . buy some more cattle?'

Sigurd looked Grimnir in the face. He looked at Olaf. Then he lowered Grimnir to the floor, and walked out.

Grimnir straightened his clothes, and glared around accusingly. His eyes strayed towards the battered old sea-chest next to Sigurd's bed-space.

* * *

It was nearly dark outside now. Loki led Olaf some distance away from the longhouse, and then looked around to make sure they were alone.

'We have to go,' he said.

'Loki, not now. We've only just come back. What's the rush?'

'They know. That thunderflash of yours has brought the earth-gods and the giants out of their caves,' said Loki. 'While Thor is without his hammer, they can range free.'

'Then we'll get the crew together, tomorrow,' said Olaf.

'No,' Loki pronounced. 'No crew. A body of men like that would be too visible. Two people only. You and me.'

'Why me?'

'You got us into this mess, you can help me to get us out of it.'

CHAPTER THIRTEEN

'Loki, I'm feeling really . . . '

'I know.'

'I only had beer and stale bread for breakfast and . . . '

'Shh.'

They had been walking since daybreak through the mountains, heading—Loki said—for Asgard, the home of the gods. As Loki had been in such a hurry, there had been no time to provide adequate food for the journey. As they rounded a dead beech tree, Loki stopped.

'I know where to get food.'

For a moment, Olaf thought he meant the red spotty toadstools that grew from the dead tree. Olaf looked at them with distaste. But Loki hadn't finished.

'There is food, but there's also a problem.'

'If there's food, there's no problem,' smiled Olaf. 'Where is it?'

'Have you heard of Thrym?'

'No, does it taste good?'

'It's not an it,' said Loki, 'it's a who.'

'What kind of who?'

'A who that's about as tall as a medium-sized tree.'

'You mean Thrym the giant?' protested Olaf.

'Shhh! He's close. I can hear him breathing.'

Olaf listened carefully for a few seconds, but could hear nothing. Clearly, Loki's senses were keener than those of mortal men.

'So how are we going to . . . oh, the . . . '

'No, no hammer. I can't risk him knowing we have it. We have to do everything by creeping around, stealing, and generally being sneaky. If he knew we had Thor's hammer, he'd do anything to get it from us. If Thrym and the other giants had the hammer, then, sooner or later, they'd attack Asgard, and chaos would come, and the great sea-serpent at the bottom of all things would swallow his own tail.'

'I know that,' said Olaf.

'So the world would end, and the sky and the sea would boil and burn into nothing. And that would be a Bad Thing.'

Olaf nodded. He couldn't help agreeing that the end of the entire world was something of a depressing prospect, to say the least of it.

They carried on for a few minutes, before Olaf became aware of a low sound that echoed round the forest, humming along the branches, and rattling the leaves. It was a while before Olaf realized that it was some kind of song, with words in it, most of which he could recognize, though they were hummed out with an odd accent.

The song seemed to go on for a long time without getting anywhere much.

'Oh, I think with my mind,
    And I sit on my behind,
    And I love to eat roasted cow.

I sit among the trees,
    Licking cow-juice off my knees,
    I sure ain't going to waste it anyhow.'

Then there was a moment when the voice went sad.

'If I could only have a wife,
    I'd be happy all my life,
    We would never have a quarrel or a row.'

Peering through the bushes and ferns into a large, treeless space, Loki and Olaf could see a huge figure, crouching in front of a bonfire. Thrym's face was so hairy that the only parts that were clearly visible were his nose and his big, black twinkling eyes. He was holding a sharpened tree-trunk, which was speared through three dead cows, and he was twisting them over the flames, and smacking his lips. Once, he held the tree-trunk over his mouth, and allowed the gobs of fat that swam out of the cows to drop into his mouth, and he smacked his lips, then sang again:

'Oh, my vest is made of leather,
It protects me from the weather,
But I can steal so I don't have to dig or plough.'

At this moment, to Olaf's horror, Loki sang out, in a piercing, female voice. It was the same tune as the giant used for his song.

'I'm a beautiful young girly,
I need someone tall and burly,
I would hug him tight and make a
true-love vow.'

Thrym rested his treeful of cows on the ground next to him, and cried out:

'Who's that?'

Loki cupped his hands around his mouth and his voice seemed suddenly to be coming from the other side of the clearing.

'Oh, just a fair young maid who needs a tall, strong husband.'

'Where are you?' boomed Thrym.

Loki's voice seemed to come from somewhere else now, a little further away.

'Over here.'

'Where?' cried Thrym getting up. 'Where are you?'

'Over here.'

The voice seemed very distant indeed now, and Thrym stood upright.

'Don't go away,' he boomed. 'I'll be right with you,' and off he went into the forest.

As soon as Thrym was out of the way, Loki and Olaf dashed to the fire, and began tearing fistfuls of meat from the roasted cows. They tossed the meat from hand to hand so as not to burn their fingers, took bites out of it and chewed furiously. Suddenly, Olaf became conscious of a rattling and a shaking under his feet. Thrym was coming back! They hurtled towards the trees.

Too late Olaf heard Loki's cry of 'Look out for . . . '

Too late, because Olaf suddenly found himself hoisted into the air by one leg. Olaf looked down from high up in a tree, not quite sure what had happened. He looked up at his leg, and saw that there was a rope looped around it.

'You have to look out for traps,' Loki shouted up to him.

By now, Olaf could hear as well as feel Thrym's footsteps, and Loki looked uncomfortably over his shoulder.

'Don't move,' Loki said, and dived out of sight into the undergrowth.

From high in the trees, Olaf watched Thrym angrily stomping back, pushing two large trees aside to get to his fireside. He sat down and picked up his cow kebab, moodily. Olaf watched in desperation, the rope cruelly cutting into his ankle, hoping that Thrym would not look up. Then Thrym looked at one of the cows, and poked with his finger, examining the hole where Loki and Olaf had removed some of the meat. He looked around suspiciously, but saw nothing, and began to chew.

Up in the tree, Olaf tried to reach up to the rope which secured his ankle, but he couldn't get a hand to it. Then he noticed the squirrel. If it *was* a squirrel. There was something just slightly odd about the eyes, and something just a little too clever and human-looking about its face. Olaf got the impression that the animal thought this was *his* tree, and he was not fond of boys who decided to hang upside-down in it. It scrabbled down his leg, and rested for a moment on his jerkin, then clambered down a little more and sat on Olaf's upturned chin, grasping at Olaf's neck with its claws, its tail dangling over Olaf's face. The trouble was that this squirrel did have a particularly bushy tail, which sent little tickly hairs into his nostrils. In fact, you might have thought that the creature was doing it deliberately.

The first sneeze just had the giant glancing round for a moment. The second, and he was intent on finding the source of the noise. With the third, he looked straight at Olaf, and roared with anger. At the giant's approach, the animal scrambled back up Olaf's body and legs, and returned to its branch. But it did not scurry off, as you might have expected. When Thrym came thumping up to Olaf's tree, it jumped on Thrym's shoulder and seemed to squeak into his ear.

Thrym pushed his face close to Olaf's, and roared. As the mouth opened, Olaf caught a glimpse of scrunched up bones stuck between yellowing teeth. Then Thrym pulled the branch from the tree. Olaf swung around helplessly, feeling (and looking) like a worm on the end of a fishing line. He looked around the forest floor, hoping that Loki had managed to stay out of sight. A few seconds went by, as Thrym examined his catch. Then Loki scuttled out of the undergrowth, indignantly, with squirrels hanging on to his hair and clothes, and scratching at his face. With one hand, he batted away at the squirriels. With the other, he clung on to the hammer.

'Loki!' boomed Thrym. 'Fancy seeing you here.'

'Let him go!' cried Loki.

'Nice hammer, Loki.'

'It doesn't belong to me,' said Loki. 'I'm returning it.'

Thrym looked down at him. The squirrels had dropped to the ground now, but stood around Loki, as if awaiting further orders.

'You can give it to me, if you like. I'll get it back to Thor for you.'

'Very . . . kind of you,' Loki said, 'but I do have to return it personally.'

'Fine. Of course, I may have to do something horrible to your little friend.'

Loki looked up and shrugged, with every sign of being completely unconcerned.

'OK. I'll be off,' he said.

Olaf was suddenly rather alarmed.

'Loki!' he screamed. But he instantly regretted it, because it was quite clear that his own little life counted for very little, compared with the prospect of the imminent end of the whole world.

'See you fellows later,' said Loki, and turned as if to go. Thrym spoke again.

'He's very squishy, isn't he?'

Loki paused a moment, before continuing to walk away.

'If I were to tread on him, it would take me a week to get the squishiness off my boot.'

Loki walked on, hesitantly.

'Now let's see,' said Thrym, 'to squish, or not to squish, that is the question.'

Loki stopped and turned. 'The boy is nothing to me. Squish away,' he said.

Thrym began to whirl Olaf around on his rope, faster and faster, now nearly colliding with the ground, now smashing through tree-branches. Then when Olaf was spinning so fast that he couldn't even have guessed which was up and which was down, Thrym hurled the branch. Rope, boy, and branch wrapped round Loki, and they collapsed in a tangled heap. The mighty hammer landed with a thud, some distance away, to be scooped up by the gleeful Thrym.

'With this hammer the giants will take over Asgard!' crowed Thrym. Then as an afterthought, he chuckled, 'But I'm going to have some fun with it first!'

And with a few giant strides Thrym took himself off into the distance.

As soon as he'd managed to get an arm free, Loki took a knife out of his belt, and began sawing at the tangled ropes.

'No chance of finding Thrym again, to recover the hammer?' asked Olaf.

'It's a big forest. No one's ever found Thrym's cave. We must go to Asgard for help. Can you walk?'

Olaf nodded, unsteadily, and Loki began walking northwards, with Olaf, bruised and aching after his encounter with Thrym, staggering at his heels. Every so often, through gaps in the trees, Olaf would catch sight of a great mountain, in the distance.

'Is Thor's palace up the mountain?'

'Yes,' Loki said. 'If we hurry, we may well reach it before the end of the world comes.'

CHAPTER FOURTEEN

The path to Asgard led through dense forest, and over craggy hills, and finally downwards into a broad valley, through which a river ran, before tumbling over a precipice. Bridging the river, and stretching upwards to a mountain that looked as if its peak had been sliced off with a huge sharp knife, was the glowing Rainbow Bridge, a luminous pathway, insinuating its way into a pair of enormous double gates which were the only visible entrance to Asgard. They stumbled up the bridge— Olaf rather nervously, because it had no supports in the middle, and looked as though it should collapse as soon as anyone set foot on it.

The gates stood slightly open, and were guarded by a bored-looking sentry, leaning on a spear. They were almost across the bridge before he noticed them, and hastily hoisted his spear to the challenge position. Unfortunately, he was holding it backwards. He looked down at the blunt end of his weapon for a moment, bemused. When he realized what he had done, he turned it round and waved it at them again. Then he recognized Loki.

'Oh, it's you. Where've you been? I haven't seen you for months.'

'How's things, Heimdall?'

'Oh, you know, pretty busy. Gets a bit hectic sometimes.'

'You do know there are giants rampaging all over the place, don't you?'

'Yeah?'

'In fact, how do you know we're not a couple of giants, in disguise?'

Heimdall's face first creased into a smile, then registered worry.

'You're not, are you?'

Loki ignored the question.

'Thor in?'

'Far as I know. I avoid him if I can.'

Loki and Olaf walked through the gates to Asgard. The palace of the gods stood, cold and enormous, surrounded by flattened rock that stretched all around it to the very edges of the mountain crags. There was an enormous portico, supported on huge stone pillars, and gigantic doors, also made of stone, supported on massive rock hinges. Of course, if the doors hadn't already been slightly open, they would never have got in at all, but since both Olaf and Loki were on the thin side, they managed to squeeze into the colossal marble entrance hall without too much trouble. Every footfall produced a chorus of echoing whispers that bounced off the rock walls and seemed to skitter along the floor under their feet. Olaf looked around, nervously.

'Now what?' he asked.

'Now we find Thor,' whispered Loki.

'What and just . . . tell him you stole his hammer?'

'Shh! Don't say that. Don't even think that. Don't even think about thinking that.'

'You mean, Thor can read my thoughts?'

'No, but I can, and you're making me nervous.'

'Sorry.'

'And don't think that either.'

Olaf had just imagined the pair of them being slammed flat by a huge fist. He was rather alarmed that Loki appeared to be able to see what he was thinking, but this did not seem the time for discussion, particularly as the hall was now echoing with something that sounded like footsteps.

Olaf tried to hide behind Loki. Loki tried to hide behind Olaf. Then they both tried to hide behind each other at the same time. A deep, booming voice banished all the smaller echoes and seemed to rock the great stone portico on its pillars:

'He who wakens mighty Thor
Must be strong in fist and claw,
For that wretch will breathe no more,
Who walks unbidden through his door.'

Olaf looked at Loki; Loki looked at Olaf.

'When the god begins to roar
And beat the terrible drums of war,
Mighty warriors tremble for
None can overcome great Thor.'

Then the footsteps started again, closer and closer. Until round the corner came . . . round the corner of the imposing marble corridor that led to the great hall, surmounted by its enormous stone portico came . . . a shortish, stoutish man with a leather apron on.

'Oh, it's you, Garram,' said Loki, almost sobbing with relief.

'Loki,' said the little man. 'Where have you been?'

'You don't want to know.'

'Well, of course I don't. You think I don't have problems of my own? Have you any idea what's been going on while you've been away?'

'Tell me,' Loki said.

'Thor had his hammer stolen.'

'Never!'

That was when Olaf noticed for the first time that Garram had a raven perched on each shoulder.

'Olaf, meet Odin's ravens, Hugin and Munin,' Loki said, by way of introduction.

'Pleased to meet you,' said Munin.

'What did he say his name was?' said Hugin.

'He didn't,' said Munin.

'Didn't what?' asked Hugin.

'Say what his name was,' said Munin.

'How can I say what his name was when I never heard it in the first place?' said Hugin.

'You see what I have to put up with?' said Garram. 'And this is all I get in the way of intelligent conversation. All his other servants have left. It's all down to me now. I mean, have you seen the mess he makes when he eats his dinner? Chicken bones, splashes of egg-yolk, crumbs as big as your fist. And His Lordship just mopes about like a troll with toothache.'

'Point is,' Loki interjected, 'is he in a good mood or . . . '

'Good mood? We are talking about Thor here. For the last seven months, all he's talked about is two things.'

'Two things?'

'Yes. The first thing he's kept going on about is what he's going to do to the thieving wretch who's pinched his hammer. And the second thing is what he's going to do to the thieving wretch who's pinched his hammer.'

Garram paused a moment.

'Actually, that's one thing, isn't it?' he said. 'But you see, I sometimes convince myself that it's two things, just so I don't go mad. In fact, if I didn't have Hugin and Munin for company, I think I'd go mad anyway.'

'Well, as it happens, Garram, we've got to go,' said Munin.

'Yes,' said Hugin, 'we have to go.'

'Why?' asked Garram. 'Why do you have to leave me on my own?'

'I can't remember,' Hugin said. 'But my powerful brain enables me to deduce that Munin and I have to carry some important news to Odin, although what the nature of the news might be has temporarily slipped my mind.'

'The news,' twittered Munin, 'is that the giants are ranging all over the country, causing chaos and mayhem.'

'Just what I was expecting,' said Garram. 'But will he listen?'

'There's more,' Munin went on. 'There's disturbances among the mortals of Skirringsvijk.'

'What?' said Olaf, suddenly taking an interest at the mention of his home village. 'What kind of disturbances?'

'I don't remember,' said Hugin.

'Well of course you don't remember,' said Munin. 'But I can remember every detail. Three men, heading off towards the market in Skirringsaal. One tall and fair, two dark and short. And the dark short ones have concealed weapons.'

'My father, with Grimnir and Egil,' said Olaf, anxiously. 'They were going to buy cattle.'

'The two dark men spoke to each other in whispers when the big man wasn't looking. But I can't think what it all means.'

'I'll soon work that out,' said Hugin. 'Or at least, I will as soon as I can remember what it was you said.'

'We're off to Odin, anyway,' said Munin. 'Good-bye, scruffy boy.'

And with that they flew off, and were soon lost in the shadows of an apparently unending corridor. Garram followed them, grumbling to himself until his voice faded in the distance. That was when Olaf noticed that one of the huge stone doors in the entrance hall was opening. Suddenly, there he was, towering above them with his beard like a forest. Thor paused when he spotted Loki. But his only response to Loki's presence was to scratch his armpits, and then sit on a rock that seemed to have been put there for the purpose.

'Loki,' he grumbled, 'where have you been all these months?'

'Well,' Loki said, 'I . . . um . . . went . . . or rather, I . . . '

'Someone stole my hammer, you know, Loki,' said Thor, in a booming voice that managed to have a bit of a whine in it. 'Yes. Stole it. When I had my hammer I was a mighty god, you know. Whereas without it . . . well, do I impress you, honestly?'

'This is Olaf,' Loki said, trying to avoid the subject. 'He's a savage from one of the villages.'

Olaf flashed an indignant look at Loki. But Thor wasn't listening anyway.

'It must have been while I was asleep. Someone must have crept in and stolen it.'

'Dear, dear,' said Loki. 'You can't trust anyone these days, can you?'

'Anyway, it's not going to turn up now, is it? I've lifted every stone in this palace, I've searched and I've searched. It's not in the palace at all. In fact . . . I think it's . . . somewhere else.'

'No!'

'I'm afraid so. Lost for ever. Lost lost lost.'

'We could try to find it for you,' Loki said.

'Ha!'

'Well, perhaps it'll just turn up.'

'I don't think so. He could have taken it any-where by now.'

'Who could?' said Loki, nervously.

'Well, you know . . . whoever it is that's taken it.'

Loki gave a little sigh of relief. Evidently, Thor had no inkling of who had caused all this trouble.

'We might just find it . . . if we could fly,' said Olaf. 'And while we're looking for the hammer, we could warn my father that—Ouch!'

Thor gave no sign of noticing that Loki had just kicked Olaf in the leg.

'Not even gods can fly,' Thor intoned.

'What about Freja the goddess?' Olaf blurted

151

out. 'Doesn't she have a magic coat made of feathers? With a coat like that, you could look anywhere you wanted. You could fly from here to, say, Skirringsvijk, in minutes.'

'Oh, that, yes, well, I did ask her but she just said if I could lose my hammer, I might lose her coat, and that was the end of the matter.'

'We'll go and see her,' said Loki.

'She's upstairs,' yawned Thor. 'See her if you want. I'm going back to bed. Oh, and be careful, she hasn't forgotten your last bit of trickery, you know.'

And with that, he was gone. Loki led the way towards the staircase. The stairs had clearly been built for people who were much taller than Loki and Olaf. They scrambled up a step at a time, using elbows and knees, and made their way along a corridor lined with ebony pillasters.

Loki took a deep breath, and rapped on the stone door of Freja's room.

'Come in, idiot!'

Obediently, Loki and Olaf pushed open the door. Everything about Freja's room was enormous, including Freja herself. She sat in front of a mirror, adjusting a gold chain around her neck, each link the size of a man's fist. Her overdress was a cataract of shimmering silk, trimmed with braid at the cuffs and hem, and embroidered with threads of real gold and silver. At her neck, her underdress was visible, fastened with a brooch of tortoishell, mounted in gold. The table in front of her had an array of bottles and boxes. This was unfortunate, because it gave her plenty of ammunition for hurling in Loki's direction. Loki kept saying things like 'Please, no, all I wanted was a quick word . . . you're looking so beautiful', except that objects kept hitting him on the top of the head, so what he was actually saying was, 'Please—ow—no—ouch—all I wanted—no, not the bottle—ow—was a quick word . . . you're looking so beautiful—ow.'

In fact, it is possible that Loki would never have survived the encounter at all, but for a lucky accident. Of course, being hit on the head with a large stone jug didn't feel like a lucky accident to Olaf. As a matter of fact, it didn't feel like anything at all, because Olaf was knocked unconscious by the blow, and when he opened his eyes again, Freja was bending over him, looking concerned, and saying that it was all Loki's fault, which, in a way, it was. But the fact that Freja was concerned about the unconscious Olaf meant that Loki could get a word in, which meant that he could calm Freja down. He was saying that he would never have dreamed of coming into her presence, but he really wanted to help this little mortal boy. This was clever of Loki, because Freja was clearly feeling a little guilty about knocking a young Viking unconscious.

'But what can I do to help? It's nothing to do with Thor and that stupid hammer of his, is it?'

'No, no, not at all. It's a sad case, Highness. The boy's father is the head man in a local village. But he's in danger—rivals plotting, that sort of thing. And the boy wants to warn him.' Olaf looked at Freja as appealingly as he could.

'Poor little mite,' she said, 'we will go as soon as the boy's well enough.'

Olaf sprang to his feet. 'Can we do it now?'

'Of course.'

'Well, that's great,' said Loki. 'If you'll just . . . hand over the coat . . . '

'Hand over the—are you insane?' screeched Freja, flinging open a stone door to reveal a wardrobe almost as big as the bedroom itself. 'No, I'm coming with you.'

'Oh, I wouldn't advise that,' said Loki. 'It could be dangerous and—'

'Loki, I have not forgotten the last trick you played on me.'

Freja clicked her fingers in the direction of the wardrobe, and the jumbled dresses and coats and skirts and cloaks stirred as if somebody was trying to struggle from among them. Then it emerged, and hovered just above the floor.

The coat was a billowing cloud of shiny feathers which flashed with gold and silver brilliance as they moved. The sleeves trailed great skeins of shimmering quills, bound together with threads of gold wire and by shining silver clasps, studded with ruby and amethyst. It hung in the air, gently undulating, as if it was anxious to begin a journey. Freja slipped in her arms, and pulled it around her. She bundled Loki under one powerful arm, and Olaf under the other, and jumped effortlessly onto the stone sill of her window.

'Ready?'

Loki looked down and was obviously not happy: 'Well, wouldn't it be better if—waaahhh!'

And they were off, at first hurtling towards the ground, then going up, up into a vast grey cloud, and out again into the sunshine. Olaf found himself looking down on a white world of clouds. There were mountains and valleys and fjords of piled cloud, stretching as far as he could see. There was such a vastness of towered and pillared clouds that

155

he couldn't tell at first that Freja was moving. Only the deafening, bone-freezing wind, tearing at his clothes, indicated that they were flying at great speed.

Olaf, gripping tight to Freja's dress, turned to Loki.

'Thanks for helping my father.'

'Help your father, hah! That was just a trick to get her sympathy,' Loki murmured. 'We're looking for Thrym. He's a giant, remember? No one's ever found his secret cave.'

'Oh, I forgot to ask,' Freja said, shouting above the noise of the rushing wind. 'Where are we going?'

'Skirringsaal,' Olaf said. 'We're looking for three men. Two short and dark, one tall and fair, heading for the middle of town.'

Freja turned, and suddenly began to fly faster. Loki, who was hanging on to Freja's dress with both hands, groaned loud enough to be heard even above the noise of the wind. Beneath them, the clouds opened to reveal the land below. They started to go even faster. So fast that the fjords and the fields and the villages were a rushing blur. When Freja finally slowed down, Olaf recognized the familiar patterns of inlets and promontories near his home village.

'There,' said Freja, pointing to a group of three dots on the ground.

'Where?' said Olaf.

'Three men on horseback. There,' said Freja.

Soon, the dots did indeed resolve themselves into mounted men. The fairest and tallest of them was some distance ahead of the others and was already entering the outskirts of the town. Grimnir and Egil (Olaf could recognize them now, from their hunched shoulders and sparse hair) seemed in no hurry, and were dawdling behind. They were leaning towards each other, as if deep in conversation.

'Can we hear them?' Olaf said. And Freja flew low, just above head-level, and far enough back to avoid any danger of being seen. After a few seconds, Olaf caught a few of Egil's words.

'Seems a bit unfair to me,' he was saying, 'but I s'pose you know best.'

'I can do business with the giants, but only if I am the undisputed leader. Got it? He has to be dead. In fact not just dead, but triple dead. Killed, then assassinated, and then terminated. And when we've finished all that, we'll do him in.'

The next few words he heard were Egil's:

'I know, I know. I just thought, maybe one death

was enough. Even Sigurd doesn't deserve to die four times. I mean, there's a proverb. "Beware the fire, when all is burnt out." No, that's not right. "You don't have to put out the fire when it is not yet burnt out." No, that's not it either. "Beware the—"'

'Who took your brother to the bottom of the ocean?'

'Well, that's true,' said Egil, 'but . . . '

'And yet he managed to come back himself. Safe and well, and brought all his fingers and toes with him. Are you telling me you don't want revenge?'

'Well, of course I want revenge. But I only want to kill him the once. Four times seems a bit vindictive.'

'How many times do I have to go over this?' said Grimnir. 'If he escapes, then he will know that someone's arranged an assassination attempt. In which case, he'll be able to turn the rest of the village against us. There must be no uncertainty. First we poison him.'

'Why don't we just challenge him to a fair fight?' Egil asked.

'Because we'd lose, idiot,' said Grimnir. 'So first it's the poison, then the knife. If he survives that, then we use the axes. And if all else fails, he'll be pushed in the river. There is no room for uncertainty. Now do you remember the plan?'

'First we buy the cattle, then we go to the . . . where do we go?'

'Then we buy a large jar of wine to take home, but we can't resist opening it, and we sit down for a while, drinking, and then Sigurd gets drunk, and when he's really drunk . . . '

'All right,' said Egil. 'You've told me all this once. I'm not stupid, you know. After that comes the knife, then the axe, then the—'

'Shhh! he can hear us,' hissed Grimnir. Without realizing it, they had allowed their horses to speed up until they had almost caught up with Sigurd, who had slowed down to get a good look at the town. With a smile, Grimnir addressed Sigurd. 'So, here we are. Skirringsaal. Let's get the business over quickly, then we can enjoy ourselves.'

Sigurd eyed him, suspiciously: 'I think I'd as soon get the business out of the way and go home,' he said. 'Strolling around Skirringsaal with a large bag of silver is like covering yourself in gravy and walking into the middle of a pack of wolves.'

'I like that one,' said Egil. 'You could make that into a proverb.'

'Shut up,' hissed Grimnir in Egil's ear. 'And if

you want a proverb, try this. "Don't believe your enemy is truly dead until he is poisoned, knifed, beheaded and drowned."'

If he could have done, Olaf would have shouted some kind of warning to his father when he found out that Grimnir was clearly planning so many terrible things for him. The only problem was that throughout the conversation, he had a large but elegantly manicured hand clamped over his mouth.

'I do apologize, little Olaf,' said Freja, 'but we always avoid interfering with the affairs of mortals.'

'Quite right,' said Loki. 'Also, we really must be getting back. Things to do, people to see, you know.'

'Then what's the point of me coming here at all?' said Olaf, as Freja hovered discreetly over the edge of town.

'Well, you've seen your father, I thought that was what you wanted,' said Loki.

'I don't want to see him poisoned, stabbed, beheaded, and drowned!' said Olaf.

'Oh. Well, I can't interfere myself, of course,' said Freja. 'Let's say you can stay here for an hour. But you must make sure your father doesn't recognize you.'

'Why?'

'Because if your father recognizes you, he'll wonder how you got here, and you'll have to tell him you had help from the gods, and that's something we don't do. If we helped one mortal, we'd have queues outside Asgard asking us to rescue cows from trees or whatever.'

'Freja,' said Olaf, respectfully, 'cows don't climb trees.'

'Really? I've never taken much interest in agriculture,' said Freja, vaguely.

'Could we get on with this? I really do have some urgent business to attend to,' said Loki. 'He's going to need a disguise. Freja, can you bring us in low over the main road?'

Buying the cattle was something of an effort. With giants encroaching on villages and farmsteads, gobbling up whole herds of cows and flocks of sheep, there was something of a shortage of animals at the moment. But Sigurd had a great deal of money to spend, and, eventually, they struck a deal with an anxious farmer eager to convert his cattle into money before it was too late. Having lived in a remote bit of Northumbria for six long years, it was a treat for Sigurd to hear so many people talking his own language. But he kept a wary eye on Grimnir and Egil. They were wandering along a street lined with market stalls when Grimnir exclaimed:

'Well, look at that, a wine stall. Perhaps we should buy some to take home.'

'If we were planning to buy provisions, we should have brought the cart,' said Sigurd, suspiciously.

'Well, we can manage one jar, surely. Tell you what, we could sit down awhile and try a little now, before we start back.'

Freja flew low over the road that led into the town, then, at a signal from Loki, swooped down and hovered just above the head of a man who was wearing a loose-fitting hooded cloak. Loki grabbed the cloak by the tip of the hood, and up they went. The man didn't notice what had happened for a moment, but then realized that something was amiss. First he patted his head, and then he put his hand on his right shoulder, then on his left. Finally he realized that his cloak was gone. He looked to the right, to the left, he looked behind, and then spun round rapidly to look to the front, shaking his fists in all directions as he did so. And of course, the only direction he didn't look was up. Loki was in fits of uncontrollable mirth. He handed over the cloak to Olaf, and off they went again, towards the centre of the town.

'I think it's time to get back,' said Sigurd. 'I'm dreeling a little funk. I mean, I'm funking a little dream . . . I'm . . . '

Grimnir winked hugely at Egil, who winked hugely back, with his one good eye, and then sat down and took a gulp of wine from the jar. Grimnir winked again. Egil winked back.

They were sitting on the edge of a cattle trough in the middle of town, at the point where the two main roads crossed. Considering it was market day, the place was pretty quiet—many were staying in their houses for fear of being attacked by giants.

Grimnir looked at Egil, irritated.

'Didn't you have something to do?' asked Grimnir.

'What, you mean, go home, like Sigurd said?'

'No, I think you might have forgotten some little job, Egil,' Grimnir said, pointedly.

'Oh, right,' said Egil. Sigurd had already started to walk away, and Egil took the opportunity to take a leather pouch from inside his jerkin, pour the contents into the wine jar, and shake it vigorously.

'Just one more drink, Sigurd, and we'll be getting back,' said Grimnir. Sigurd hesitated, but he was not one to turn down the offer of a drink, even from Grimnir. He turned round, rather unsteadily, and came back to the cattle trough where Egil and Grimnir were sitting.

'There's hardly any left,' Grimnir said. 'You might as well finish it.'

Sigurd raised the jar to his lips, and was about to drink deeply, when a figure, looking like an old man, with the hood of his cloak pulled low over his face, crashed into him, dashing the jar from his hands. The jar fell, colliding with the edge of the cattle trough and smashing. The remaining wine formed a rich, purple pool in the mud.

Sigurd ran a few steps after the hunched figure, shouting indignantly, but couldn't catch him. He was amazed by the speed at which this old character could shift.

'Never mind,' said Grimnir, taking Sigurd's arm and leading him down towards the river, 'we'll have a little stroll round the town.'

'No, we're going home,' Sigurd said. 'We left the horses up the other way, didn't we?'

'They'll be fine,' said Grimnir. 'Relax. Enjoy your day out. You go on ahead. Egil and I will saunter on behind.'

'Why not?' said Sigurd, suddenly feeling much more relaxed, as the wine soaked more and more thoroughly into his brain. 'You don't go to the big town every day.'

'That's right,' said Grimnir.

'You know what?' Sigurd said. 'In spite of everything that's happened, I like to think of you two as my friends.'

'Exactly,' said Grimnir, 'and we're very fond of you, aren't we, Egil? In fact, why don't we all hug each other?'

'Good idea,' said Sigurd, his voice cracking with emotion. He held out his arms. 'Come on. Big hug.'

'Not here,' said Grimnir, taking a knife from his belt. 'Let's all have a big hug in that narrow little alleyway.'

'Yeah,' Egil said. 'This way.'

And so Sigurd stumbled towards the alleyway, a little fish-smelling ginnel between two longhouses. Egil opened his arms, welcomingly, and Sigurd stumbled over to embrace him, leaving his unprotected back an easy target for Grimnir's knife. Grimnir prepared to aim for the heart. And that was when the cloaked figure came hurrying through the alleyway, cannoning into Egil and Sigurd, who in turn stumbled backwards into Grimnir, who overbalanced and tumbled to the ground. His knife clattered from his hand, and was scooped up by the cloaked figure, who then hurried off.

'He's got your knife!' Sigurd cried. 'Don't worry, I'll get him for you.' But the figure had gone now, and after running a few stumbling steps out of the alleyway, Sigurd gave up.

'Never mind,' said Grimnir. 'We'll head for the river, and have a look at the waterfall.'

'Good idea,' said Sigurd. 'You know something? You two are my best friends in all the world. I mean, you, Egil, you may be missing a finger or two, and a few toes, and some teeth. And an eye. But what's left of you is pure gold.'

Grimnir removed a wickedly sharp little axe that was tucked into the back of his belt. 'The path is a little narrow here,' he said. 'Why don't you walk on ahead? Don't worry, I'll be right behind you.'

They were in a deserted little street now. Sigurd stumbled ahead, supported by Egil, who held him at arm's length so that Grimnir could get a good swing at his neck. Grimnir pulled back the axe and prepared to strike. But suddenly the axe was tugged from his hands. He turned to see a cloaked and hooded figure hurrying off ahead, towards the river.

'My axe!' shouted Grimnir.

'I'll gefinitely det him for you this time, I mean, I wefinitely dill . . . ' Sigurd said.

'I can buy another one, I suppose,' snapped Grimnir, through gritted teeth. 'Let's go and look at the waterfall.'

Already they could hear the rushing water, but the waterfall was difficult to see properly from the bank of the river.

'You have to lean right out,' Grimnir said.

Sigurd leaned. And he suddenly found himself tumbling into the water, just above the falls. It was almost as if he'd been pushed in the back. There was no escaping the drop. Though he tried to fight it, the current was dragging him nearer to the brink. Head down he plunged, towards the foaming rocky base into which the torrent poured, when he felt a tug at his jerkin, which stopped him in mid-descent. A cloaked figure, who had evidently climbed out onto a branch overhanging the waterfall, had caught hold of him with both hands.

'Will you let go of me?' said Sigurd indignantly. 'You're tearing my jerkin, you imbecile.'

But there was no response. Sigurd was swung to and fro, then fro and to, in bigger and bigger arcs, until, finally, he was released, and sent spinning over onto the riverbank. As he lay there panting and wet and muddy, Sigurd picked up a nice round stone that was sitting in the slime. He weighed it in his hand, and then hefted it at the retreating figure on the opposite bank of the river. Considering his inebriated condition, his aim was remarkably true. The stone hit the cloaked figure squarely on the back of the head. There was a surprisingly youthful-sounding cry of pain as he disappeared into the trees.

At last, Olaf reached the little field where Loki and Freja were waiting. He was gasping for breath after all his exertions, and when he had discarded the cloak he rubbed the back of his head, carefully.

'All done?' asked Freja.

Olaf didn't have enough energy to do anything but nod. Without a word, Freja scooped up Loki and Olaf and rose into the air. In moments, they were back among the piled and drifted billows, with a biting wind in their faces. Soon, looking down, the purple-green haze of the forest could be seen through a cloud-ravine.

'It's cold up here. Could we fly a little lower?' asked Loki.

Obligingly, Freja dived down over the trees that filled the valley, not far from where Olaf and Loki had encountered Thrym the forest giant, and then swooped off again towards Asgard.

The thunderbolt came unexpectedly, from a dense place in the trees, and whistled and fizzed up into the rainclouds. Freja screamed indignantly, and flew down towards the source of the fireball. On a tree-studded hillside, almost invisible from every direction, was a huge cave, and dancing in front of it was a large hairy giant, holding a shining, and very impressive, war-hammer. It flashed again, but Freja was ready this time. She swept sideways out of the way of the thunderbolt, and then up over the grey clouds, and found a quiet pool of air. For a few seconds, all was still. Then Freja growled:

'What's going on?'

'Going on?' said Loki, all innocence.

'Shall I drop you on your stupid skinny bottom, or your stupid fat head?'

'Freja,' whined Loki, 'you wouldn't do that.'

Without a word, Freja opened her left arm. Loki dropped, shrieking, into the gulf between the white clouds. Olaf looked at Freja in horror, then down at Loki, who was now just a black, wriggling speck.

'All right, better catch him, I suppose,' said Freja.

And with that, they swept down through the drifting clouds. Freja scooped up the gibbering Loki, and headed skywards once more.

'I'll tell you everything. Anything. What do you want to know? Please give me a chance.'

'The hammer. It was you, yes?'

'Yes,' squeaked Loki. 'Please don't tell him. I'll be your friend for ever.'

'All right,' said Freja. 'You can stay alive. For now.'

Without another word, she flew down over the

mountains, and lowered them onto a crag in front of the palace, then jumped into the air once more, her feathered coat rustling in the mountain breeze, and disappeared into her own upstairs window.

CHAPTER FIFTEEN

'Well, the good thing is,' said Loki, 'and this is the bit I want you to remember—we know who's got your hammer and where he is.'

Thor danced about with delight, and the stones in the palace walls rattled and shook.

'On the other hand,' Loki continued, 'the person who has got it is . . .'

'Yes?'

'Thrym the forest giant.'

'Thrym who's almost as big as me?'

'Well, yes.'

'If it had been anyone else in the world, I could have punched their head off.'

'Quite.'

'I could have flicked their head off with one finger.'

'Well . . . yes.'

'I could have *belched* their head off.'

'Probably.'

'In fact, I could have . . .'

'Yes, yes,' interrupted Olaf, hurriedly.

'So, what's the plan, Loki?' Thor asked.

'Well. What we need to do . . . the thing to do is . . . we'll . . . well, actually, I don't have a plan.'

Thor cried out in anguish.

'I have . . . sort of a . . . plan,' Olaf said.

Thor and Loki looked at him.

'Well, not a plan as such, more . . . the beginning of an idea.'

'Go on.'

'Well, from the little I know about him, I'd say that what Thrym really wants more than anything in the world . . . is a wife. There's a rhyme . . . how does it go . . . ?

> *Thrym the forest giant, with boots as big*
> *   as houses,*
> *Wants a plump and comely wife to mend his*
> *   coat and trousis*
> *But why would any woman in the kingdoms*
> *   of the Norse,*
> *Want a husband with the manners of a*
> *   badly-brought up horse?'*

'Yes, yes, so what's the plan?' asked Thor.

'I think I see what Olaf's getting at,' said Loki.

'All we need is to find someone who'll marry Thrym, and swap the wife for the hammer, and we've done it.'

'Brilliant,' said Thor. 'Excellent, boy. Let's go and see him now and . . .'

'Of course, the only problem is,' Loki interrupted, 'that in order to do that, we need to find an attractive woman—perhaps a goddess—who doesn't mind being married to a disgusting smelly giant.'

Thor said, 'H'mmm.'

Then Loki said, 'H'mmm.'

Then Olaf said, 'H'mm.'

Of course, they were all thinking of the same person, but no one wanted the job of asking Freja to marry Thrym.

'Tell you what,' said Loki, 'we'll all go up there.'

This time the stone jar hit Thor, and a shower of smaller objects rained on Loki. Olaf was more wary now, and hid behind Thor, but he had to dodge around to avoid the shower of fragments that bounced off the other two. When Freja had stopped throwing, Thor said, 'So what do you think, will you marry Thrym so I can get my hammer back?'

The problem was, of course, that once the table was empty, there was nothing left for Freja to throw except the table itself. Luckily, they managed to duck in time, and the bits of wood that rained down on them only resulted in a few cuts and bruises. When the last fragment had crashed to the floor, Thor said, 'So, that's a no then.'

Freja would probably have begun pulling the stone from the walls and hurling it at them, but Olaf piped into the silence:

'Of course, it doesn't actually have to *be* a woman.'

All eyes turned on him.

'It could be . . . almost anyone. As long as Thrym *thinks* it's a woman.'

Loki thought for moment. 'So we just . . . '

'Exactly,' said Olaf.

'Exactly what?' said Thor.

'Don't worry, it'll suit you, Thor,' Loki said. 'After all, you're roughly the same dress size as Freja.'

The dress fitted quite nicely, and as Thor himself remarked, his legs were a good shape, if a little on the hairy side. Freja found a veil to cover his bristling beard and with a little eye-liner and eye-shadow, he could flirt behind the veil like any blushing maiden.

They all shared a gigantic meal of beef and veal and mutton and venison and bread, which had been set out in the Great Hall, and then made their way down the mountain. There were now two servants, for Garram had persuaded Gullveig to join them. She was a big-boned, strong-wristed woman who was only too happy to escape the constant heat of the kitchens. Olaf was glad she had come. She was plump and friendly-looking, and seemed to laugh a good deal. Thor was already wearing his dress, and he kept tripping on the hem, and stumbling. At the base of the mountain, a special covered cart had been prepared, with curtained windows, and a cushioned interior. This was for Thor to ride in. Harnessed to the front were Thor's pet goats, Gap-tooth and Crack-tooth.

'In you go then, Thor,' said Loki, indicating the cart.

'Excuse me,' Thor replied indignantly from behind his veil. 'That is no way to talk to a lady.'

Of course, the big problem was that Thor was extremely heavy, and refused to walk even short distances in case he caught his dress on a thorn-bush. He just sat in his cart, with an ornate polished mirror in his hand, looking at his face and practising fluttering his eyelashes. So it was necessary to stop every twenty minutes for the two exhausted goats to rest. Also there were tree-roots and stones and holes, so there were many pauses so that the cart could be lifted over obstructions. On top of all this, Gap-tooth and Crack-tooth refused to go at anything faster than a very leisurely pace, so that they could nibble at grass and leaves and pretty well anything else that came within reach of their mouths. Then the going got tougher.

'Not that I'm complaining,' said Garram as they shouldered the cart through a particularly dense bit of forest, 'but couldn't he just walk for a bit? Until we get closer to . . . wherever we're going? I mean, would it kill his ladyship to . . . '

At that moment, there were three loud thumps on the roof of the cart, and everyone looked round in shock at three squirrels, sitting there defiantly with evil looks in their small black eyes. Garram reached up to knock one of them off, and then yelped as it sank its small yellow teeth into the soft skin of his wrist.

Some laughed, and some jumped back in alarm. Garram shook and shook his arm, but the squirrel hung on. It was Olaf who held the squirrel by its body, then squeezed its jaws until the mouth

178

released poor Garram's flesh. Olaf threw the squirrel up into the branches, where it skittered around angrily. With two energetic leaps, the other squirrels joined him. They scrabbled and (it seemed) whispered for a few seconds, then bounded off out of sight.

Loki said, 'Ratatosk.'

'You mean squirrels?' Olaf enquired.

'Oh, they look like squirrels, of course. But they are members of the Ratatosk. Thrym's spies. Things are working out rather well.'

'Oh, working out well, is it?' Garram said. 'And me with my hand almost chopped off by the wild beasts of the forest. I mean, here I am, wounded, perhaps fatally, mortally wounded, and will I get any thanks for all this? After all the pain and suffering and the . . . '

Big-boned Gullveig came over to examine the wrist.

'Here,' she said, and pulled some leaves from her apron. 'Self-heal. I was saving it to put in a drink, but . . . ' And she squeezed the little leaves until a few drops of the juice landed on the wound.

'Better?'

Garram nodded, uncertainly. Gullveig looked around a moment, then went to a nearby shrub, a brownish one with prickly branches, and small purple flowers. Holding out her hands as if she were holding a skein of wool, she carefully extracted a spider's web from the shrub, then wrapped it around the injured wrist.

Garram opened and closed his fingers, experimentally. He was evidently in less pain now.

'One more thing I need to ask you,' said Gullveig.

'Yes?'

'You married?'

Garram raised his eyebrows and coughed. Gullveig burst into laughter and gave him a slap on the shoulder that sent him stumbling into a tree, then went to the back of the cart to push it over the bumpy ground.

'I'm not sure whether I'd rather be savaged by a wild animal . . . or looked after by Gullveig. The effects are about the same,' Garram grumbled.

On they went until sunset, when they found a fern-carpeted clearing in the midst of dense pine forest, where they decided to stay for the night. Olaf wondered what they were going to eat, since no one had bothered to bring any food. Then Garram emerged from behind the cart, loaded down with joints of meat to roast by the fire.

'Where did—' began Olaf. Then he realized what had happened. 'Not Gap-tooth and Crack-tooth?'

'They may be rubbish when it comes to pulling carts,' said Garram, 'but nicely roasted, I think you'll find them delicious.'

CHAPTER SIXTEEN

Olaf woke from a dream of being kicked in the ribs by giants, to find that he was being kicked in the ribs by Gullveig.

'Ow!' groaned Olaf. 'Warrisit, wassamarrer?'

But by the time he had woken properly, Gullveig was standing motionless in the glow of the fire, frozen in the action of pointing out into the forest. Olaf instantly regained consciousness, and looked around. On every twig of every branch of every tree; on every rock and every lump in the ground, a tiny pair of eyes shone. They shone, not with reflected light, sending out a little beam that illuminated the place where the eye pointed. It was of course the Ratatosk. Olaf started to walk towards Loki, who was just beginning to rouse himself, but some of the beams lit up Olaf's face, and at that second, it didn't seem to matter what happened any more. He became conscious that some of the Ratatosks' eyes were edging closer, but he simply stood there and let them come.

Without warning, something hit him, hard, on the back of the neck, and he screamed out with pain. There was Loki, standing just behind him with a branch, and the most likely explanation for the sudden exploding pain was that he had just been hit on the back of the neck with it. He was about to grab the branch and wallop Loki back, when he realized that the Ratatosk had drawn very close, and that he had only allowed them to do this because the beams of their eyes had somehow sent him into a sleepy stupor. He turned to Loki.

'Come on,' Olaf urged, 'weapons.'

But already Loki's eyes were glazed, and he watched the approach of the Ratatosk with a stupid smile fixed to his face. Olaf punched him in the mouth as hard as he could.

'Thanks, Olaf. You couldn't manage one more could you?'

Olaf punched him again.

'Splendid, thanks. Yes, that's done the trick. Where are the weapons?'

'Hidden under Thor's cart. There's no time!'

The little orange eyes got closer and closer. It seemed as if there were hundreds of them, and as they watched, Olaf and Loki could feel themselves slipping again into sleep.

'We've got to do something,' Loki said, drowsily.

'Yes,' Olaf agreed.

'If we just stand here talking, they'll kill us all.'

'Exactly,' said Olaf.

'Talking and talking,' Loki said. 'Definitely not something you should do when you're in danger.'

'That's right. A time for action, not talk.'

This could have gone on until the Ratatosk sank their teeth into Olaf's and Loki's flesh, but all at once, Olaf had a moment of sanity. He slapped his own face, kicked himself in the shin, and shook himself. He thought about weapons. In sheer desperation, he felt around on the ground near his feet and made contact with something heavy and hard. It took a moment for Olaf to work out what it was. Then he remembered that Thor had killed his two goats so that all could have an evening meal. These must be the goats' bones! Grasping a big thigh-bone, Olaf looked up at five pairs of evil little eyes, and took a swing. With a surprised 'Ooooh' five Ratatosk squirrels went sailing up into the air.

'Quick, Loki, they'll get you,' he squealed seeing more of the little creatures closing in on Loki. But Loki moved not a muscle. One of them sprang into the air and fastened its claws on to the neck of Loki's tunic. A pair of white teeth flashed in the dark, and moved fast towards Loki's neck. But not fast enough to avoid being whacked by Olaf's goat-bone.

With a tiny squeak of rage, the Ratatosk flew across the forest.

'Loki, here!' shouted Olaf. But Loki had drifted back into unconsciousness. Olaf swiped him on the back of the head.

'Ow, thanks,' said Loki, who picked up another leg-bone and set to work. With a few swift movements, Ratatosk were flying in all directions, with little angry squeals that faded into the distance.

'It's no good, they're coming back,' Loki shouted. Olaf threw a goat-bone at Gullveig, which caught her square on top of her head and shook her out of her torpor. In a flash, she picked up the bone and began swinging left and right. For a moment it seemed that she would be able to deal single-handedly with the Ratatosk problem— but only for a moment. With alarm, Olaf realized that Gullveig had frozen in mid-swing, and that Loki, too, had stopped fighting. It was at this point that Olaf had one of his better ideas. He ran to Thor's chair. Thor was sleeping in it, staying upright so as not to crease his dress, and in his hand was the mirror into which he had lovingly gazed for the entire previous day's journey. Olaf ran back to Loki's side. The Ratatosk were advancing again, hundreds of eyes, in row upon row, getting closer and closer.

Olaf held up the mirror. For a short time, the advance continued. But after a few moments, some of the eyes stopped moving. Olaf slowly swung the mirror in an arc, so that every pair of wicked eyes was reflected back to its owner, and eventually all movement stopped. The Ratatosk had sent themselves off to sleep, and tiny snores could be heard all around.

You might have expected Thor to be grateful that someone had saved him and his followers from being torn to pieces by the Ratatosk, but instead he was annoyed. First because his mirror had been borrowed without his permission, and second because one of the goat-bones was missing. Olaf couldn't understand why Thor was worried by this, until Gullveig explained things to him.

'They're special goats,' she said. 'They'll come back to life in the morning sure as anything . . .'

'But only if not one bone is lost,' Thor whined.

'I've eaten that goat seven hundred and sixty-two times in the last year alone. It's been fried, boiled, spiced, roasted, and stewed. First my hammer, now my goat. And it's all your fault,' he whined, looking at Olaf.

Olaf thought this a little unfair, but began searching around, as did everyone else. It was a large thigh-bone that was missing, so it shouldn't be difficult to locate it. The problem was that although the sky was now lighting up a little, it was still hard to see anything on the ground. Also, no one was sure when the snoozing Ratatosk would wake up and start looking for some flesh to sink their teeth into.

'Tell you what,' said Olaf, 'I'll tie some rags around this stick, dip them in oil and use it as a torch.'

(The rags later turned out to be a particularly attractive pink veil that Thor was saving up for the wedding, and the oil was perfume, also put aside for the big day, but no one noticed this until it was day-light, and much too late). Olaf took the torch to the fire, and lit it with the glowing embers. It worked well, throwing a wide circle of light wherever he moved. But though he walked up and down, down and up, right and left, and left and right, he could not see the missing bone anywhere. When the torch went out, Olaf put it to the ground and stripped the rag from it with his boot. That was when he noticed that his torch was made, not from a stick and some rags, but from a bone and some rags. Olaf had been using a goat's thigh-bone as a torch in order to search for a goat's thigh-bone. He was wise enough not to say anything except, 'Found it.'

He placed the bone in the appropriate place on the ground, with the other bones. By now it was getting lighter, and Olaf watched with interest to see what would happen next. It started with a slow movement of the skull, as if it was just rocking from side to side in the breeze. Then the skull rolled upright, and paused long enough for Olaf to wonder if anything else was going to happen. Then it gave a little jolt, and hopped on top of its own jaw-bone. Then skull and jaw slowly rose into the air, to hover at goat's head level. The skull looked to left and right out of its empty eye sockets, and opened and closed its dry-bone mouth fast, as if it was laughing. And then every bone began to move in a small circle, under the grinning head. And one at a time, a big bone or small would find its proper place and jump to it, then bone would climb or leap on bone until the goat had a back end with legs and a front end with legs. Then the vertebrae lined themselves up and began to march in single file up to the goat's front legs, where they were encouraged in their climb by a nudge from the goat-skull's horns. Up they climbed, making their way one at a time across the head, and joining with each other to make a perfect spine-bridge. Then the ribs came, impatient, leaping up the nearest leg to fasten onto the backbone, until there stood a complete goat skeleton. It took a few experimental steps—a little unsteadily on the leg that had been singed while being used as a torch—and then it stood and waited as muscle and sinew and ligament and cartilage and eyeball, then skin and whisker and goat-beard and tail grew as Olaf watched. The goat, Olaf thought, gave him a rather evil look—as if he knew who had scorched his front right thigh bone, but as long as it didn't learn to talk, Olaf reckoned he didn't have much to fear.

The going did not get any easier as they went deeper into the forest, but it did feel safer now. The Ratatosk had evidently decided to treat them with a little more caution after the last encounter, and though there was the occasional distant detonation of a thunderbolt, the close-packed trees around them meant that there was little danger of anyone actually being hit. Eventually they came to the side of a huge, pine-fringed lake, where Thor and his retinue stopped.

When they had rested for a short time, Loki said, sleepily, 'Oh, Olaf, did I tell you about your job?'

'Job?'

'You didn't think you were coming along for the pleasure of it, did you? No, you're going to have to earn your keep.'

Olaf didn't like the sound of this.

'Well, surely you've worked it out,' Loki said.

'Worked what out?'

'Thor has no lady's maid.'

'What?'

'Well, obviously, Thor is going to need someone to do his hair, and make sure his dress doesn't get muddy, and help him with his make-up . . . '

'What!!!???'

'Well, who else is there?'

'What about Gullveig?'

'Not ladylike enough. No, the dress will fit you much better.'

Until that time, Olaf himself had never realized the extent of the colourful language he had picked up after living his twelve years in a Viking village. He used some of it in his reply to Loki, and though it is not possible to report the exact words that he used, he made it clear that he had no intention of dressing in girl's clothes.

'OK,' Loki said calmly. 'You can do it dressed as a boy then.'

It was only a few minutes later, while he was being instructed in exactly what his duties were to be, that Olaf realized that he had been so busy objecting to the idea of wearing girl's clothes that he had neglected to object to being made into any kind of bride's helper. But by then, of course, it was too late to do anything about it, and Olaf had to spend an entire evening being instructed in picking up the hems of long dresses while walking through mud, and applying cosmetics to the eyes, and brushing and styling of hair.

That evening, just before sunset, they did their first parade along the beach, Thor wiggling his hips and fluttering his eyelashes over a bright pink veil. And Olaf had to walk behind, stooping to support the dress over the puddles and mud-patches. But Giant Thrym did not put in an appearance during the performance, and they prepared to camp for the night. Garram and Gullveig had built some little ragged brushwood shelters by the lakeside, and before they crawled in through the tiny doors, Olaf and Loki turned to watch the sun sink westwards into the lake.

That sunset saved their lives, for it was only because they were pausing to admire the orange-streaked sky that they avoided being blown to pieces as the thunderbolt crashed into the huts. There was a flash and a loud noise, and Olaf became aware of a wonderful feeling—as if he was flying through the air. After a moment, he realized that the flying-through-the-air feeling was caused by the fact that he was flying through the air— luckily in the direction of the lake. Poor Garram was flying far ahead of him, for he had been the closest to the place where the thunderbolt struck, and it looked as if he was destined for the very centre of the lake.

'Now I ask you, is this fair?' he grumbled, as he tumbled over the water. 'Do you call this fair?'

The coldness of the water would have taken Olaf's breath away, if he had had any, which he didn't, because he had breathed out during the explosion, and what with all the excitement, he hadn't got round to breathing in again. When Olaf made it to the cold surface, he took a deep gulp of air, looked around and saw the other members of his party flailing about in the water. The problem was that there was a large person waiting for them on the lakeside. Giant Thrym, clutching the twinkling war-hammer, was belching out volleys of laughter as he watched them struggle for the shore. Olaf wasn't sure what to do—whether to strike out into the lake and risk drowning, or head for the shore and risk being flattened by Thrym. So he turned to look behind him. A long way off, poor Garram was being towed to shore by Gullveig. Nearby, Thor was floundering in the water. Olaf grabbed at his sleeves, and pulled him towards the shore. Thor was a heavy burden to tow through the freezing water, but after a minute or so it was shallow enough for them to stand upright.

On the shore, Giant Thrym was just about to unleash another thunderbolt, when he caught sight of Thor, striding out of the water. Thrym was twirling a medium-sized pine tree in one hand, and waving the war-hammer around with the other, but the sight of the figure in the dress emerging from the waves stopped him in mid-twirl. His grip loosened on the hammer. He made a soft noise at the back of his throat. Soft for Thrym, that is.

'Ohhhjjjjkkk!' breathed Thrym adoringly.

Thor straightened his dress, and tried to arrange his veil in an alluring fashion. Thor wriggled his hips. He batted his eyelids. He shook his head from side to side so that his hair fanned out in damp, dark tresses.

'Can I . . . er . . . help you out, dry your clothes, brush your hair, marry you?' Thrym gasped out in one sentence.

'Why yes,' said Thor. 'How about now?'

'Well,' stumbled Thrym, 'I have a battle to go to right now.'

'Of course, a lovely girl like this won't stay single for long,' Loki urged.

Thrym hesitated. He had obviously been looking forward to using the hammer in a real battle, but a chance to marry such a beautiful and willing maiden was not to be missed.

'Tomorrow,' he pronounced. 'I'll have to get ready for the wedding first.'

'Of course, there are certain conditions,' said Loki.

The giant's eyes gleamed with recognition.

'Loki,' he said. 'And your little squishable friend. What are you doing with this beautiful girl?'

'She's . . . my sister,' Olaf said. 'And she can't marry you unless you agree to make a couple of promises.'

'What promises?' Thrym boomed.

'A new outfit every month.'

'Done.'

'And . . . er . . . just a teeny thing this, but she would like that war-hammer as a little engagement present.'

'Oh, I'm not sure about that.'

'So you don't love her then?'

'Oh, it's not that, it's just, well, this is a special hammer.'

'She's a special girl,' said Loki, with a glimpse at Thor, who was wiggling a finger in his ear to clear the water out.

Thrym's mouth flapped open and shut. Of course he wanted this vision of loveliness to be his wife, but on the other hand, the hammer had given him so much fun.

'I'll let her borrow it some time.'

'OK, how about now?'

The giant was in agonies of indecision, but suddenly he made his mind up.

'No. She can borrow it. For a few moments only. On our wedding day, and not before.'

The wedding was fixed for the next day, and Thrym lumbered off, happily. No one had the heart to start building new shelters, so each found a warmish place among ferns and furze to rest. Olaf found a willow-shaded patch close to the lakeside. It had been a long day, and it was good to relax, letting the warm breeze dry out his wet clothes. Then, as he looked up into the sky, a couple of birds appeared, coming in over the forest from Asgard. Odin's ravens!

Soon they were gliding in, landing at the water's edge to drink after their long journey.

'News,' Hugin said, when they had done with drinking. 'We have news.'

'News?' Thor repeated—rather stupidly, Olaf thought.

'Not just news,' croaked Hugin. 'Very important news. Vital news. This news is urgent, essential, and significant. Added to which, it is of extreme consequence.'

'Well, what is it?' asked Olaf.

'Dunno. Can't remember,' Hugin said.

'The giants are approaching Asgard,' said Munin. 'The hammer must be returned soon, or all is lost.'

'You can tell Odin that all is in hand,' said Thor. 'Is that all?'

'Almost,' said Hugin. 'We also have news for the mortal boy. You know, whatsisname.'

'The boy Olaf,' added Munin.

'Me?' said Olaf.

'We flew over your village yesterday. Odin wanted us to check up on the activities of a certain mortal who has been consorting with giants,' Munin said.

'Grimnir,' Olaf breathed.

'Nah, my name's Hugin,' said Hugin, 'can't you remember anything?'

'Not you, him,' said Olaf, exasperated.

'Not me him what?' said Hugin.

'Can we get on with this?' interrupted Munin. 'A frost-giant was having a conversation with this Grimnir.'

'Well?' asked Olaf.

'The giants have managed to make the Protecting Spell,' said Munin. 'For many years they have sear-ched for traces of Balder's blood, and by scraping and collecting, and grinding and distilling, they have gathered three pure drops.'

198

'Doesn't sound like much,' said Olaf.

'It's not,' said Munin. 'Not enough for a giant to use. But for a skinny little mortal man like that Grimnir, it's just enough to do the trick. He drank a potion made with Balder's blood, and now he is guarded by the Protecting Spell.'

'The Protecting Spell?' said Olaf, puzzled.

'That's right,' said Hugin. 'And with the Protecting Spell, my mighty brain tells me that even such a one as Grimnir might be a threat to man and gods. You see, it's a . . . a . . . well . . . you tell them, Munin.'

And Munin chanted the spell, in the sing-song voice that magicians use.

> *'Nothing made of flesh or bone,*
> *Not earth nor mud, not soil or stone.*
> *No plant that grows from earth or dirt,*
> *Not one of these can do him hurt.'*

'I think Grimnir is preparing for a challenge,' said Loki.

'What? I have to go and warn my father,' Olaf said.

'No time now,' said Loki. 'Ragnarok is at hand, remember? When the hammer is recovered, then you can go.' Olaf saw the sense of this, but he was uneasy, realizing that Sigurd was now in even greater danger, and that if the spell did indeed give such sweeping protection as it promised, then Grimnir would be a merciless opponent.

'Thank you,' said Loki. 'You can go now.'

'What, with no supper?' said Hugin. 'And us flown here all the way from . . . from . . . from wherever we just flew from?'

'All right. Stay for supper,' Thor said. 'I'm hungry, anyway.'

In fact, suddenly everyone was ravenous. Being blown up and thrown into the middle of a lake has that effect. Thor looked around, and there were his goats, cowering at the edge of the forest.

Thor was delighted, and called out softly to the animals.

'Come on, don't be frightened, I'm only going to kill you.'

CHAPTER SEVENTEEN

The cave in which the wedding was to be held was at the foot of a wooded hill some miles from the lakeside camp, through ground that was by turns boggy and overgrown. Even Thor had to admit that riding in a cart was impossible in this terrain, and they left it by the lakeside. Olaf trailed dutifully behind Thor, while Loki walked with a sprightly step, and sometimes gambolled—probably, Olaf thought, with delight at the sight of Thor proudly striding along in his bridal outfit, while Gullveig, who had washed herself and tidied her clothes, looked neat and pretty, in spite of her tall stature and muscular frame.

The wedding was to be in the evening, and by the time the hill came in sight, the light had faded somewhat; but the cave was easily visible, because Thrym had surrounded its opening with torches. As the company drew closer, they could see that the inside was decorated with bluebells, cow-parsley, and willow-herbs, giving it a bright and homely aspect. Olaf almost felt sorry for Thrym, who had taken so much trouble and was obviously looking forward to having a wife to share his lonely forest. Thrym, spruced up in his best cow-skins and beaming with pleasure, thumped out to meet them. Thor pulled at the veil to ensure it covered his bristly beard, and fluttered his eyelashes, flirtatiously. Thrym took Thor's hand and led the party into the cave, where, on a table made of twenty-five sturdy oak trees strapped together, a huge feast was laid out. There was a large quantity of meat on plates and trenchers and on dishes so big you could have put to sea in them. There was meat turning on spits, and roasting and toasting in front of fires. Then there was the fruit. There were apples boiled in honey, and cherries soused in wine, and sweetened plums bubbling and boiling over slow fires. Then there was the drink. There was mead and wine and ale in buckets and bowls and bottles and barrels, and if you wanted more, outside there was a vat the size of a small lake brimming with spiced mead and wine.

And it could only be assumed that Thrym had prepared all this almost unaided, because the only help he had was from the little Ratatosk squirrels, for it was they who turned the spits and stirred the vats and stoked the fires with forest twigs.

Gullveig looked at Thrym in admiration.

'Handsome giant, bin't he?' she said to Olaf.

Olaf looked at her to see if she was joking. She wasn't.

'The marriage,' said Thrym.

'In good time,' Loki said. 'First, the feast. Come.'

'Let the bride eat first,' Thrym said, with a shy look at Thor.

Thor took a boat-sized dish of meat. He turned around, lifted the veil, and emptied the entire contents of the dish into his mouth, and swallowed. Next he picked up two spits on each of which was a roasted cow, and into his mouth they went. Thor smacked his lips greedily and looked round for more.

'I have seen many strange things and people,' Thrym said, 'but never have I met anyone, man or woman, who could eat so much in so short a time.'

'Well,' Olaf said quickly, 'the thing is, that she was so looking forward to meeting you on her wedding day, that she hasn't eaten anything for a week.'

'Very well, perhaps my bride would care for a little drink,' Thrym simpered.

Thor did not need to be asked again. With one hand he grabbed a vat of mead from the table, carefully lifted the veil just enough to get it to his mouth, but without revealing his black bushy beard, then raised it to his lips, and gulped it down.

'Well, well,' said Thrym, suspiciously. 'What a thirsty girl.'

'Ah, yes, well,' Olaf stammered, 'she was so looking forward to meeting you on her wedding day that . . . she hasn't drunk anything for a week.'

'I see,' said Thrym, a bit more doubtfully this time, 'well, if my little bride has done eating and drinking, then perhaps she would care for a big kiss from her bridegroom.'

Thor froze in horror. Olaf piped in quickly, 'Well, she would be delighted,' he said, 'but first, she would like to see your mighty war-hammer.'

'You naughty girl, I can't do that.'

'But you promised,' Olaf reminded him.

'Oh, very well. But just for a moment. It's under the table. Kiss first.'

And without pausing for an answer, Thrym grabbed at the veil and lifted it. He was already puckered up for a kiss, but he soon unpuckered when he caught sight of the lower half of Thor's face.

'She . . . a b-beard,' stammered Thrym.

'Oh, yes,' said Olaf, 'you see, she was so looking forward to meeting you on her wedding day . . . that she hasn't shaved for a week.'

Giant Thrym looked from Olaf to Thor, from Thor to Olaf, and he roared with indignation, realizing the trick that had been played on him. Thrym seized Thor by the throat, and Thor grabbed Thrym by the shoulder. Thrym snarled in Thor's face, and Thor snarled back. But neither of them could move, because they were so equally matched in strength that each froze the other to the spot. Then Thrym grabbed Thor by the ear and pulled, and Thor cried 'Ouch!' and tweaked Thrym by the nose.

'You are like all the air-gods, feeble, and cowardly, and what's more,' said Thrym, 'your bum looks enormous in that dress.'

'What!'

Each grabbed the other by the neck, and they circled. Then Olaf had an idea. He ducked under the table. Sure enough, glittering in the faint beams of torch-light, was Thor's war-hammer. He dragged it over to where Thor and Thrym were circling.

'Thor,' said Olaf.

'Don't bother me now,' said Thor, 'I'm busy fighting.'

'But your hammer,' said Olaf.

Thrym grunted. 'You heard what the man said, we're busy fighting, now leave us.'

'But your hammer,' said Olaf.

'Leave me alone,' said Thor. 'If I don't defeat him I'll never get my hammer back.'

'But . . . '

Instead of trying to speak again, Olaf placed the handle of the hammer in Thor's hand. Thor looked at Thrym. He looked at the hammer. He looked at Thrym again. Then he gave a triumphant roar, and there was a flash. The great oak table split from one side to the other, and everything slid to the ground. There was another flash, and a large hole opened up in the wall, wreathed in the smoke of the thunderbolt. Thor strode out triumphantly. As he followed, Olaf looked back at poor Thrym, huddled in the corner in a shocked and disappointed heap.

Thor tore off his bride's outfit. Under the dress, he was wearing his own black leather garments. An elegant broadsword swung at his belt, and he tossed the hammer from side to side, and laughed hugely.

'I'm hungry,' shouted Thor, and he called his

goats, which bounded down from the hillside towards him.

Olaf turned to Gullveig.

'Are you hungry?' Olaf asked.

'I can't eat for thinking of that poor cheated giant as was looking forward so much to having a bride,' Gullveig sighed.

'Come with me,' Olaf said.

Soon, Olaf and Gullveig were back at the cave. Olaf stood at the entrance and shouted.

'Can we talk to you?'

'No!'

'Even if there's a woman who wants to see you?'

'Don't believe you.'

'It's true.'

'Does she have a beard?'

'No.'

'Let me see.'

Shyly, Gullveig stepped to the middle of the cave-mouth.

'Does she want to trick me?'

'No, she wants to marry you.'

'What, an ugly old giant with bad teeth?'

'You bin't ugly,' Gullveig said, 'and I love bad teeth.'

'Come in a minute then.'

Olaf waited outside patiently, and the noise of subdued talking went on for some minutes.

'Will you marry us?' Thrym boomed.

Olaf wasn't sure whether a small Viking had the power to bind people in marriage, but it seemed rude to refuse.

He stepped in. Thrym and Gullveig were already standing side by side.

'We're ready now,' said Gullveig.

'OK. But it'll have to be quick. Do you take this smelly old giant?'

'I do,' Gullveig said.

'And do you take this woman?'

'Yes please,' said the giant.

'I now pronounce you giant and wife. You may kiss the bride.'

The giant did.

Olaf grabbed some sliced meat from the spoiled wreckage of the marriage feast, and pushed it down the front of his shirt. As soon as he was outside, he took to his heels, and caught up with the rest of the party.

'Loki, I have to help my father,' said Olaf, 'but before I go . . .'

'You want to thank me for all I've done? You want to express your affection for me?'

'No, I just wanted to know . . . which way is Skirringsvijk, exactly?'

'Downhill from this path,' said Loki, pointing across an endless tract of undergrowth. 'Keep going until you hit the ugliest bit of Norway you could possibly imagine, and you're there. Good luck.'

Olaf headed off through the wind-rippled ferns at a brisk walk. He travelled for the rest of the night, and then continued through the day, stopping only to sleep fitfully for a few minutes under dew-dripping trees, and to bolt down some of the meat he had brought with him. There were a few steep ascents to be made over mountain tracks, but most of the journey was downhill, towards the sea. He eventually came out on a piece of sparse, rabbit-cropped turf that sloped down to a wave-tormented beach, but it didn't look familiar, and he wondered for a while if he had somehow ended up miles away from his intended destination. But there was a headland, just visible from the beach, that looked familiar, and he headed for it.

He soon saw Skirringsaal a little way off, but he knew he had to go past it to get to the muddy patch of coastline where his own village stood.

Something had happened to Skirringsaal. There was a gap in the row of longhouses, like a missing tooth. It was as if a giant boot had stamped down on it. Olaf shuddered and carried on, but the evidence of devastation was everywhere. Tree-trunks stood shattered and branchless around the fields.

There were mossy banks just a little way up from the sea. Of course, Olaf had no intention of actually going to sleep, but he decided that after such a long journey, it wouldn't hurt just to sit down. Then when he'd sat down, he thought maybe it wouldn't be a bad idea to rest his head briefly, and now he came to think of it, perhaps just closing his eyes for a moment would be a good way of making sure he was in tip-top condition, ready for any . . .

Olaf was aware of two things. First, there was about a pint of saliva running down from his mouth, and second there was a head, looming above him. He wiped away the saliva, grunted, and closed his eyes again. That was when someone slapped his face. Olaf opened his eyes, and realized that the head belonged to Loki. There was a noise, which gradually resolved itself into a stream of words, not all of them printable. Then Loki said:

'Another one?'

Olaf nodded, and Loki delivered another stinging slap on the cheek.

'What are you here doing?' Olaf asked, when he had finally regained enough consciousness to put the words into more or less the right order.

'Thought you might need some help. You know, with fighting, surviving . . . waking up.'

'Thanks.'

'Shall we go?'

'Mm,' said Olaf. 'You want some beef?'

He fished around in his jerkin, and managed to recover a couple of slices that were stuck to an area just above his belly-button.

'I'll manage without, thanks.'

By the time they were nearing the jetty where the *Skuldelev* was tied up, it was possible to hear the buzz of an excited crowd. They both ducked low, and headed up towards the enclosure, where everyone in the village seemed to have assembled, forming a massive ring.

Most of the sounds of the crowd were either 'Ooh', or 'Aaah', although sometimes there were five or six 'Ooohs' before an 'Aaah' would break the monotony. Something was clearly going on, but with the tight-packed spectators blocking the view, it was difficult to tell what. Then there was an even bigger 'Aaah' than the previous six, and a collective intake of breath. The circle opened, just to the right of where Loki and Olaf were watching from the cover of a straggly little bush, and someone was carried out. It was Harald, and his head lolled back as four members of his family carried him towards their house. With a shock, Olaf realized that Big Harald was now Dead Harald, which seemed a bit of a shame. Olaf would have trusted Harald with his life, and there were few others in the village whom Olaf would have trusted with his bootlace. There was time before the ring closed back in on itself to see what was going on inside. Grimnir was standing there, calm and untroubled, and Sigurd was squaring up to him, swinging his sword around expertly.

It was obvious what was going on. Having become invulnerable to mortal weapons, Grimnir was in the process of winning the leadership of the village by single combat. Normally, if it came to a fight between Grimnir and a butterfly with a dodgy wing, Olaf would have backed the butterfly. But if Grimnir had managed to overcome Harald, then the spell was clearly working.

'What are you going to do?' asked Loki.

'I hadn't really thought,' Olaf whispered. 'Or

rather, I just vaguely had this idea that I'd warn my father and then we'd leg it away from the village. I think now I'll have to do a Brihtric.'

'What?'

'You know, shout werrggghh, use sword, crack many skulls.'

'If Grimnir is invulnerable, then you can't really do anything to him,' Loki pointed out.

'I know.'

'That's what "invulnerable" means, when you think about it.'

'So what do you suggest?'

'How about you ride into the enclosure, grab your father, and then head for the mountains?'

'Excellent plan,' said Olaf. 'The only slight flaw is that I don't have a horse.'

'I may just be able to help you there. But before I go any further, I have to tell you something. Remember Balder.'

'What?'

Sigurd was floundering, but he clearly had no intention of giving up. Both eyes were swollen and bruised where they had been battered by the butt-end of Grimnir's sword. The sleeves of his jerkin were in shreds, and blood was dripping down both wrists. He was limping not just with one leg, but both, which did not make for great balance as he slashed and thrust at Grimnir, who nonchalantly stepped aside at each of Sigurd's attacks, and casually delivered another debilitating wound.

Sigurd had lost his shield and dagger, and there was obviously no chance of recovering them, since Grimnir had tossed them to the other side of the enclosure. Grimnir was using a shield and a broadsword, and had managed to bruise most of the bits of Sigurd that weren't already covered in cuts. Weak with exhaustion, combined with plain amazement that Grimnir was managing to beat him, Sigurd sank to his knees, and waited for the end.

That was when the wolf appeared—if you can call something a wolf when it's around the size of a full-grown bull, and can leap effortlessly over a crowd of spectators, even when it has a twelve-year-old boy riding on its back. The wolf paused for a moment, surveying the scene, before running twice around the arena, scattering the terrified spectators to the corners of the enclosure. Then it came to rest next to Sigurd.

'Climb on!' urged Olaf.

'Do you mind?' said Sigurd. 'I'm trying to fight here.'

'Father, I have to get you out of here. You can't win.'

'That's defeatist talk,' said Sigurd trying to rise from his knees, only to fall forward onto his face. 'I think I nearly had him that last time.'

'Father, please. He can't be hurt. Climb on.'

'I'm not leaving now,' said Sigurd, painfully rising to his knees again. 'I'm just getting into my stride.'

Grimnir was approaching.

'Father, now!'

'No!'

'Oh, all right then, you leave me no choice.'

That was when Sigurd noticed that Olaf had a large piece of wood in his hand. Olaf swung it round hard, and hit Sigurd on the back of the neck. He collapsed, face first. The wolf crouched, and Olaf slid off and hauled the dead weight of his father onto the wolf's back. Grimnir approached, uncertainly, but Olaf was back on before he got within sword-range. The wolf gave a howl like ten thousand hungry children discovering that their dinners had been burnt, and hurtled across the enclosure towards the opposite fence. More observers scattered, and the wolf bounded off into the forest, in the direction of the mountains.

They were halfway up the mountain, and making good progress now, although they'd had to rest for some hours before Sigurd had recovered enough to balance unaided on Loki's back.

'Just a couple of hundred cuts and bruises. Nothing to worry about,' he said, although he was still occasionally leaning against the wolf for support.

'So this big wolf thing is actually Loki?' Sigurd asked.

'Exactly.'

'And Loki is actually a god, right?'

'That's right,' Olaf said.

'So when is he going to change back into Loki again?' Sigurd asked.

'I was just wondering that,' said Olaf. 'What do you reckon, Loki?'

'Owwww—ow—ow—owwwwwww!!!!!' said Loki.

'Are you going to be like that for a while?'

'Owwww—ow—ow—owwwwwww!!!!!' said Loki.

'I think he's having trouble changing back,' Olaf said.

'Owwww—ow—ow—owwwwwww!!!!!' said Loki. He lifted his big wolf-nose as if he were sniffing the air, and then pointed his head further up the mountain. There was a large figure, striding up towards the peak. A very large figure. In fact, a giant. And on his shoulder sat Grimnir, desperately hanging on for support to the giant's distended earlobe.

'They're using him in the battle for Asgard,' said Olaf.

'Who, the giant?' said Sigurd.

'No, Grimnir.'

'Grimnir!' said Sigurd. 'I could beat him with one arm tied behind my back!'

CHAPTER EIGHTEEN

Sigurd gazed in awe at the rich glow of the distant Rainbow Bridge. Beyond it were the walls of Asgard, around which clouds of dust and smoke hung in the air. The battle for Asgard, it seemed, had already begun, and it sounded as if Thor was making good use of the mighty hammer. For some time, the sky had been lit with flashes, and the air riven with rolling roars of thunder. The massive walls were already in a sorry state, with huge ragged gaps all the way along. The gates were pitted with holes and leaning over crazily.

As they drew closer, several large, coarse heads appeared over the battlements. The giants were inside the walls of Asgard! One of them snapped off a chunk of wall and flung it into the distance. It crashed with a thump that shook the ground under their feet. In response, a thunderbolt fizzed through the air, and struck the wall next to the giant, who roared with pain, and disappeared from sight. Olaf and Sigurd grabbed handfuls of fur to hang on to, as Loki bounded through the forest that lined the Bifrost River around Asgard.

Thor was encamped behind a pile of hastily-felled trees.

'Ah, Loki,' he said, having no problem at all in recognizing the wolf, 'bit of a problem, I'm afraid.'

'Owww!' said Loki.

'By the time I'd got back, the giants were already in.'

'Oww—owww!' said Loki.

'But we have a surprise lined up. Just wait until Freja gets here. We'll show them then.'

Sigurd, already awe-struck at the sight of the Rainbow Bridge, and the towering walls of Asgard, simply stood goggling at Thor, who absent-mindedly handed bows and arrows, first to Olaf, then to Loki. He seemed to have forgotten for the moment that a wolf might have a problem using that particular weapon, and he didn't seem to have noticed Sigurd's existence at all. Olaf handed Loki's bow to his father. A volley of rocks cascaded all around them, kicking up soil and debris from the forest floor. When they had all dusted themselves off, and recovered their wits, Thor squinnied once more into the distance.

'Ah,' he said, 'here she is.'

Freja was indeed approaching, in a gold chariot, pulled by two large . . .

'Cats!' Olaf exclaimed.

'Eh? Well, yes, she has cats to pull her chariot. I thought everyone knew that.'

The cats were huge, but otherwise exactly like the skogkatts that were kept as pets in many longhouses.

'I think you're going to have to hide, Loki,' said Olaf. 'They don't like the look of you.'

Growling indignantly, Loki backed off behind the remains of a shattered tree, and Freja and her cat-drawn chariot pulled up close to them. One of the huge cats put its head down. At first, Olaf thought it was going to gobble him up like a mouse, but then the throaty purring noise betrayed the cat's intentions. It wanted to be stroked! Olaf rubbed the shaggy fur, and looked up at Freja, who was deep in conversation with Thor. So this was the terrible surprise they had in store for the giants. A couple of oversized skogkatts!

'What happened to all the other gods in Asgard?' Olaf asked.

'Locked in by the giants,' sighed Freja. 'I only escaped because I was away, visiting a . . . gentleman friend.'

221

'You mean, Odin is in there . . . ?'

But Thor and Freja weren't listening. They were gazing into the trees in the direction from which Freja had come. Out of the forest came a beautiful woman. Her hair was long, and dark, twisting in lustrous ringlets down her shoulders. As she approached, the beauty of her face and eyes became more apparent. Olaf gazed at her. A fly buzzed into his open mouth, but he barely noticed it. The beautiful woman's skirt was split at the sides, and as she walked, her legs protruded. It was only when she had drawn closer that Olaf noticed the maggots. In and out of the grey, lumpy flesh of her legs, a thousand little pink and white wriggling bodies writhed as she walked.

'Oh, Hel!' breathed Olaf.

'Exactly,' said Thor. 'Freja has brought the dark goddess from the nether world, together with her cohorts.'

That was when Olaf saw the grey shapes marching in silent unison behind the terrible goddess. Faces and arms like grey putty, a grim army of corpses strode on towards Asgard. Hel herself headed into the shadows of the forest—back, Olaf guessed, to her dark kingdom. The soldiers of Hel were armed as they had been in life. As they grew closer, a company of archers broke away from the main group and began to loose their barbed arrows. Others set up huge catapults. The remainder continued to advance, and were met by a steady hail of projectiles, hurled at them by the giants. Struck by the mighty rocks, the attackers were horribly damaged, but a little thing like a missing arm or leg didn't stop them. They marched or crawled on relentlessly. Soon the siege catapults began hurling back the rocks which the giants had flung earlier. One of the phantom soldiers had his head struck off by a flying boulder, but managed to stay upright long enough to add his own head to the pile of rocks in the catapult, and it was flung, along with the rocks, over Asgard's battlements.

There was panic behind the walls as the rocks slammed down, and several giants shouldered their way out of the huge gates. The Rainbow Bridge shook as they tramped along it, each clutching an axe whose newly honed edge glinted in the red light of the setting sun. Thor led Sigurd and Olaf forward, and Freja followed slowly. The cats didn't seem too keen on getting close to the fighting. Thor unleashed more thunderbolts at the enemy, while Sigurd and Olaf loosed arrows as they went. Some of the thunderbolts detonated on the bridge, hurling giants into the river, far below. Some hit the giants in the middle of their flabby torsos, flinging them backwards onto the ground. One giant was hit in the neck, and stood headless for a few gruesome seconds before crashing to the earth with a thud that could be felt as well as heard. As soon as they came within range, the Army of the Dead flung their spears in cruel arcs that found many a lumbering target.

'Easy!' crowed Thor. 'Keep going.'

Freja stood up in her chariot, and drew back an elegant gilt recurved bow. The deadly arrow sprang forward, and buried itself in the heart of the foremost giant. There was still a steady rain of missiles from the giants, who needed no catapults. In addition, Olaf spotted two black shapes bundling over the walls towards them.

'I'll get them,' Sigurd said, levelling his bow. But the arrow went wildly askew when Olaf knocked his arm out of the way. Just in time he had recognized the shapes. Not some ghastly new weapon of the giants, but Hugin and Munin.

'We've got out,' said Munin.

'That's right. We've escaped from . . . where did we actually escape from?' said Hugin.

'We've come to help in the battle,' Munin said. 'Now what do you want us to do?'

'How are you with a club?' asked Thor.

'Never joined one,' said Munin.

'What about bows?'

'We don't wear them,' said Hugin.

'You're no good to me,' growled Thor. 'Just keep out of the way.'

The army of the dead was tramping over the Rainbow Bridge now, swarming around the giants, hacking at them with swords and axes. Several crashed to the ground under the onslaught, and soon Hel's army was ready to pour through the gates of Asgard. Thor gave a bellow of triumph, certain now that the day was won. That was when he became conscious of a swelling noise behind them. It was a high chirruping sound, combined with the thump of heavy footsteps. Olaf looked around and, to his horror, there was Thrym, stomping towards them from the direction of the forest, accompanied by what looked like a huge, red, moving fur rug.

'What in Thor's name . . . ?' said Sigurd. 'Begging your pardon, Your Thorship, what can that—?'

'Ratatosk,' breathed Olaf.

Hugin squawked, and took to the air.

Munin followed.

'Miserable cowards,' cursed Thor.

Olaf didn't blame the ravens. Never had he seen so many creatures in one place. Acre upon acre of chattering Ratatosk squirrels were advancing on them. The soldiers of Hel who had stayed behind to shoot arrows and man the catapults were now writhing on the ground, overwhelmed by the Ratatosk tide. Loki howled, and bounded off in their direction, and soon his wolf jaws set to work, clamping the little rodents between his powerful jaws and tossing them into the air. But even a huge ferocious wolf could not deal with them single-handed. On they came, hissing spitefully. Olaf and Sigurd loosed a few arrows into their midst, but it was difficult to tell whether they found their mark, so huge was the approaching tide of red fur. Soon the Ratatosk were massing all around them, and Olaf and Sigurd had to sweep them aside using their longbows. Onto the bridge went the Ratatosk and began to engage Hel's soldiers, swarming up their legs and battening on their rotting fingers and faces. The putrid battalions dropped their weapons, and staggered around blindly, their faces swathed in twitching fur. Hemmed in by the cruel Ratatosk from behind, and the giants from the front, they either fell or leapt over the parapets of the bridge.

'To Hel with you!' roared a giant from inside Asgard's walls. And back to Hel, Olaf supposed, was exactly where they were going.

But there was no time to think about that now, because in addition to the continual bombardment of rocks, flung by the giants, the Ratatosk squirrels continued to torment them. One leapt at Thor, and clung to the collar of his jerkin, raking at his chin with his sharp little claws, before being batted away by Thor's clumsy fist.

Then the ravens came. Olaf recognized Hugin and Munin out in front. Behind them, a great black cloud of flapping feathers. They swooped down and scooped up the squirrels by their tails, then dropped them into the swirling waters of the Bifrost River. The relentless ravens worked tirelessly, swooping and scooping, then dropping their hissing burdens into the gorge.

'Now's our moment!' screamed Thor. 'Forward!'

Thor brandished his hammer, and released a thunderbolt which smashed into Asgard's battlements. He ran towards the bridge, and Olaf and Sigurd followed, still kicking and swiping at the vicious little vermin that leapt at them from all

227

directions. Freja urged her chariot-cats forward, and they began to advance, very slowly, mewing pathetically. Olaf took a look back. Most of the Ratatosk were in retreat, harried by their aerial attackers, and Thrym had turned tail, pursued by ferocious wolf-Loki. Olaf followed Thor onto the bridge, followed by Freja, who had been untroubled by the Ratatosk. The cats may not have been keen on getting too close to the battle, but their teeth and claws were more than a match for small furry mammals. They left a trail of little mangled bodies as they advanced.

Six giants stood on the bridge as they approached. Two were felled with thunderbolts, and a third struck with arrows until he ran, yelping, back through the gates. The others were swept aside with direct blows from Thor's hammer. With a scream of triumph, Thor, followed by Olaf and Sigurd and Freja, made for Asgard's gate. Soon the giants inside would surely be at their mercy. Then a figure emerged from inside. Not a knobbly, muscly giant, but a small, thin man, holding in his hand a short sword.

'It's Grimnir,' said Olaf. 'Thor, we have to be careful here. Don't use the . . . '

Too late. Thor unleashed a thunderbolt that

sizzled towards Grimnir's unprotected head. Grimnir barely flinched. The thunderbolt stopped, a hand's width from his body, and gave a pulsing flash before bouncing back towards the wielder of the hammer. Thor ducked, and the thunderbolt fizzed on into the forest, felling a swathe of trees before slamming into a distant mountain. Thor stood amazed. Once more, he pointed the hammer, and again the thunderbolt hit an invisible something in front of Grimnir and fizzed back, this time colliding with an unfortunate raven, who quite simply evaporated, leaving only a quiet puff of smoke and a couple of black tail feathers behind.

Then the rocks began to pour down once more, to the accompaniment of scornful howls from the giants on the battlements. Thor backed off, and Freja's cats, whining as fragments of rock pinged off their small pink noses, retreated. But a chariot is not designed to go backwards, and soon it was wedged between the parapets of the bridge, cutting off any hope of retreat. Grimnir stepped forward, whirling his little sword. Thor was not used to being bested in a fight. He was too confused by the failure of the hammer to do its work to do more than stand there, looking at the jewel-decked weapon in dumb amazement. So it was Sigurd who met Grimnir's attack. He managed to block the sword-swipes that Grimnir aimed at Thor, but when Sigurd tried to counter-attack, his furious swipe merely shattered his sword-blade. When he attempted to use what was left of his sword to block the next attack, Grimnir's blade made painful contact. Sigurd sprang back, and looked down at his injured hand, which was now missing two fingers. Olaf was there to deal with the next sword-blow, but he only succeeded in deflecting the blade, which slammed into the side of Sigurd's head. Sigurd dropped to the ground, and casually Grimnir advanced, ready for the kill.

Olaf, suddenly fired with anger, advanced on Grimnir, and swung his blade in a wide swipe at Grimnir's head. The pain in his wrist as the sword connected with the invisible barrier was agonizing. All Olaf could do was drag Sigurd back and haul him into the pink-cushioned interior of Freja's chariot. All this happened under a constant bombardment from the battlements.

Thor lifted the stricken war-wagon with a tearing, wrenching sound as the wheels scraped on the parapets, and set it down facing the other way. Freja—still standing at the reigns—cursed at Thor for the damage he was doing, but Thor ignored her, and soon she was urging the cats to move. In spite of the fact that their harnesses were twisted crazily around their legs, and the damaged chariot wheels swung from side to side on their axles, the animals moved faster now that they were running away from the battle rather than towards it. There were screams of derision and triumph from the giants as the stricken vehicle waddled and wobbled back to safety.

Loki was waiting for them at the makeshift camp.

Humiliation had made Thor furious.

'It must have been some freak accident,' he growled, 'I'm going back there to finish the little pipsqueak off. Who's with me?'

'I'll come,' said Sigurd, groggily, waving his damaged hand around before collapsing back on the ground, unconscious. By now, Freja had procured bandages, and she and Olaf began to bind up Sigurd's wounds.

Loki howled and whined, desperately: 'Owww, ow-owwww!'

'Grimnir's protected by a spell,' Olaf said, carefully winding a bandage between Sigurd's thumb and the remains of his forefinger. 'That's what

Loki's trying to tell you. There's nothing we can do.'

'Protected from what?' thundered Thor.

So Olaf chanted the rhyme-spell to Thor.

Loki seemed to get excited. He bounded around them, making little yapping noises. But Thor wasn't paying any attention.

'What was it? Nothing made of flesh or bone. So animals can't hurt him.'

Loki was rushing around excitedly again.

'Quiet, Loki,' roared Thor, 'I'm trying to think. Now what was the next bit? "Earth or water, soil or stone . . ." Can't get him with a rock then.'

Loki was actually nibbling at Thor's ankle now, and Thor kicked him away irritably.

'What was the next thing?' asked Thor.

'No plant that grows from earth or dirt,' said Olaf.

At this point, Loki went into impatient fits in his bid for their attention. He bounced around them; he yelped; he lay wriggling on his back, and jabbed his paw up towards the tops of the trees.

'Behave yourself, Loki,' said Thor, 'I'm trying to think.'

But Loki carried on, in the same perplexing way,

as if he were holding something with one of his paws, and then pulling at it with the other. The trouble is that wolves are not noted for their skills in the art of mime. The action Loki was doing could have signified pulling a branch out of a fire, or drawing a sword from its sheath, or drawing back a bow. On the other hand, it could have meant taking a halibut out of a bucket, or removing a turnip from the hat of a very short man. Thor looked at Loki for a moment, puzzled, then continued with his thought.

'No plant. So nothing made of wood. Also he can't drown, since he's proof against water.'

'Exactly,' said Olaf. 'There isn't anything that isn't rock or soil or water or animal and all plants grow out of the ground. You see? There's nothing we can do.'

At this Loki started to bounce around again, jumping in the air and nipping at Thor's nose. Thor fanned him away ill-temperedly, then gave him a gentle kick. Of course, a gentle kick from Thor was enough to send him flying through the air. Loki landed on his feet, some distance away, and then started to lope off into the forest.

'Loki!' Olaf shouted. 'Don't disappear. We need you.'

The shouting woke Sigurd up.

'Don't worry, I'll get him for you,' he said, climbing to his feet then falling immediately back again onto the ground.

'Who exactly are you?' Thor said abruptly, apparently noticing Sigurd for the first time.

'This is my father, Sigurd,' said Olaf. 'Father, this is Thor.'

'Yes, my lord,' said Sigurd, reverently, 'I recognize you from the rock-carvings. If you ask me, they don't do you justice.'

'They always do me from the right,' Thor said. 'I've always thought my best side is from the left, but will they listen . . . ?'

Wolf-Loki returned, with a few twigs in his mouth, which he dropped at Olaf's feet.

'Loki, will you stop that?' Olaf said, kicking the sticks aside.

'Owwww!' said Loki.

'Loki, go away,' said Thor, 'I'm trying to think.'

But Loki wouldn't go away. He stood over the pile of sticks, panting and howling and nosing at them. Olaf picked them up to examine them.

'Mistletoe,' he said, looking at the white berries.

'Very pretty,' said Thor. 'Now, Loki, get out of the way.'

'Just a minute,' Olaf said, 'before he started this wolf thing, Loki said something about . . . ' And then Olaf smiled to himself.

Olaf approached the Rainbow Bridge armed only with a bow and some freshly made arrows. He was an easy target for the giants, but though the rocks rained down, none of them hit him. Any rock that might have been a danger was shattered in mid-air by Thor's thunderbolts. On Olaf went, all the way to the bridge.

Grimnir looked at him with contempt and then slowly drew his sword. Olaf retreated a couple of paces, and then raised his bow. Grimnir just continued advancing. Olaf pulled a tiny arrow from his belt, and set nock to string. Grimnir raised his sword in preparation for a downward swipe. Olaf pulled back the bow, and sent the little arrow flying at Grimnir's shoulder. Grimnir continued advancing, adjusting the angle of his sword to get the maximum effect. But then his face registered alarm. Something was wrong. He looked down at his left shoulder, and there, lodged deep in the flesh, was a tiny arrow. A trickle of blood was already discolouring his jerkin. He looked up at

Olaf, and then back at the arrow, evidently trying to work out what had gone wrong. He tried to remove the spiteful little barb, but by that time Olaf was ready to loose a second dart, which caught him in the back of the hand. He gave a little squeal of pain, and flapped around, looking for a means of escape. He dropped his sword, and rushed past Olaf, still tugging at the tormenting darts. Taking careful aim, Olaf loosed yet more spiteful little arrows that lodged in his neck, his back, and his buttocks. As each barb struck, Grimnir gave another shriek, but he was soon lost to sight, and fleeing deep into the forest.

Olaf was too exhausted to help much with the re-taking of Asgard. But to tell the truth, once Grimnir was dealt with, he was not really needed. Two massive detonations took the gates off completely, and then Thor strode in, sending thunderbolts to right and left, and the earth shook as giant after giant crashed to the ground. Soon the surviving giants were in full flight, falling over each other in their haste to cross the Rainbow Bridge and run back to their homes in Jottenheim.

* * *

Once all the excitement was over, Loki managed to regain his true shape, and he walked back into Asgard on two legs, rather than four. Thor released the gods from the hall into which the giants had herded them, and they streamed out, gratefully. Only one god was missing, which, in a way, was not bad going. But the missing god happened to be a rather important one.

'Where is Odin?' said Thor, worried. No one knew.

So the corridors and passages, the kitchens and storerooms, the cellars and boiler-rooms were searched. But when Olaf saw two large black birds disappearing into an open window in a distant part of the palace, he smiled to himself, and led Sigurd along a pillared corridor. On the way, he explained how, with Loki's help, he had managed to break through Grimnir's protective spell.

'It's like the story of Balder,' Olaf explained. 'He couldn't be hurt by anything of the earth, or anything that grew out of the earth, but there is one plant that doesn't grow out of the earth . . . '

'Mistletoe!' said Sigurd, rubbing at his aching hand. 'It grows from a tree.'

'So I just had to tip some arrows with mistletoe,' bubbled Olaf, 'and . . . '

Sigurd nodded. And for the first time in his life, Olaf felt that maybe his father was at least a little proud of him.

They travelled down a long corridor at the end of which was a pair of enormous wooden doors. With difficulty, Olaf swung one of them open, and they made their echoing way down a dark and statue-lined hall. At the far end of the hall was a seated figure, with a pet raven on each shoulder. He was looking down with great concentration at a runic chart.

'It's Odin,' jabbered Sigurd.

'Yes, father.'

'Olaf—that is Odin the all-father, greatest of all the gods.'

'Don't worry, he's fine when you get to know him.'

Olaf and Sigurd bowed respectfully, but could not conceal their amazement at the calm scene before them. Odin hadn't even noticed their presence, so deep was his concentration on the symbols.

'What on earth . . . How did you . . . What has been going on here?' Olaf said. 'How can you be so calm after all the fighting and noise and upheaval?'

'I don't remember,' said Hugin.

'I can't think,' said Munin.

'What upheaval?' said Odin.

CHAPTER NINETEEN

Olaf and Sigurd were invited to stay in Asgard for as long as they liked, but both felt that they should get back home as soon as possible. Besides, there was a good deal of work to be done in Asgard that they couldn't really help with. Clearing up the huge scattered rocks, not to mention a good many dead giants, would not be a job for mortals. Especially a twelve-year-old boy, and a man with two missing fingers.

They had more or less decided to sneak away, a couple of days later, when the weather was promising and they both felt rested and ready for the journey. They were making their way out of the stone portal when Thor and Freja appeared, followed by Loki. All smiled and lifted hands in farewell gestures.

'I have gifts,' Thor said, presenting Sigurd with a ring made of rare and precious red gold. To Olaf he gave a jewel-studded short-sword.

'Call on me when you fall in love and want your

marriage blessed,' Freja said. 'I'll make sure you have fifteen children, all strong boys.'

Olaf blushed, and turned to Loki.

'I think life will be a little dull without you around,' he murmured.

And slowly, Olaf and Sigurd crossed the Rainbow Bridge, back into the world of mortal men.

Names and places in this book: a guide to pronunciation

Balder (*bal-der*):
Before his cruel demise, Balder was often on the receiving end of some fairly childish humour. People would frequently ask 'balder than who?' or mispronounce it as 'bladder'. Needless to say, they all felt bad about teasing him, after his untimely death.

Brihtric (*brit-rick*):
Part of a well-travelled family of Angles, with a relative in China called Rick Shaw, and Irish sharp-shooting cousin Rick O'Shea.

Egil (pronounced *egg-ill* as in a breakfast that's feeling off-colour).

Freja (*fray-ah*):
This means 'high-born lady'. The name is appropriate. After all, she is a lady, and she was born in Asgard at the top of a mountain, which is about as high as you can get.

243

Garram (*gah-ram*):
The stress should be on the first syllable. Getting the pronunciation of this name right is all about stress. In fact, since he works for Thor, Garram's whole life is about stress.

Gullveig (*guhl-veeg*):
The first syllable rhymes with 'bull', which is what she's built like.

Grimnir (*grim-near*):
The pronunciation is very appropriate as life gets grim if you live anywhere near him.

Jarnsaxa (*jarn-sax-ah*):
A giantess whose name means 'iron sword', which was what people called her to her face. Behind her back, she was known as 'the old battle-axe'.

Jottenheim (*yot-un-hime*):
Or to put it another way *yacht-un-hime*. Spelling is weird, don't you think? If a sailing boat is *a yacht*, then a baby's bed is *cacht*, and the thing you're sitting on right now is your *bachttom*.

Harald (*harr-ald*):
Try saying the word 'Herald', only change the initial vowel to an 'a'. Alternatively, just say 'Harold' the English way, which will produce an identical sound anyway.

Hugin:

Pronounced *hoo-gin*, with a hard 'g' sound as in 'begin'. Hugin is a deep thinker and has spent a good deal of time pondering what his name might mean. After several thousand years of serious consideration, he managed to work out a profound significance in the way his name was spelt. Unfortunately, as he has no capacity for memory, he had forgotten the whole thing by the following Tuesday.

Kveld-Ulf (*quelt-oolf*):

Remember to pronounce this carefully, especially if Kveld-Ulf is present. Even some of his Norse contemporaries had trouble saying it at times. They found it even more difficult after he'd taken the tops of their heads off for mispronouncing his name.

Loki:

Pronounced *low-key*, which is the way Loki wants to keep things at the beginning. During the story, Loki's life goes into a higher key until by the end, he's downright off-key.

Munin (*moo-nin*):

Pronounced *moonin*, and yes, he is given to showing his bottom in public places. Fortunately a raven's bottom is not a very rude object, being covered in tail feathers, so this causes little offence in Asgard, where he lives.

Odin (*oh-din*):

His Irish descendant, Patrick Flaherty Wills O'Din pronounces his name in almost the same way as the Norse people did, only with slightly more stress on the second syllable.

Rattatosk (*ra-ta-tosk*):

An aggressive sounding name for something as fluffy as a squirrel. The name has a musical sound— like the smart rapping of a snare drum. None of these squirrel-like creatures has, as far as can be established, ever played the drums, although a famous ratatosk family some centuries ago boasted three oboists and a mandolin player.

Sigurd (*Sih-gourd*):

Some seed-pods are called gourds. These are in no way related to Sigurd.

Thor (*thor*):

As someone with a lisp once remarked, this is an apt name. He usually acts like a bear with a thore head, and if he loses his temper, you could end up feeling thore for a week.

Thrym (*Thr-im*):

A small name for such a large giant, you may think. Actually, it's a little joke that giants share among themselves that a small giant has a big name and vice versa. As you can probably tell from this, giants have a very poor sense of humour.

Valholl (*val-hurl*):

Many people wrongly refer to this as 'Valhalla', which is actually a plural, and would suggest that there are several halls where the souls of departed Vikings fight, swear, and sing rude songs all day. Believe me, one Valholl is quite enough to annoy the neighbours.

Wulfruna:

Pronounced *wool-froon-ah*. She is better known than her sisters, Cottonfruna, Mohairfruna, and Acrylicfruna.

Names mentioned in Snorri's story

No one has ever managed to work out how the names in this story are pronounced, for the simple reason that no one has ever stayed awake for long enough.

When he's not writing stories and poems for children, Martin works as a freelance teacher, story-teller, and actor. He has also written television comedy and radio drama. Martin enjoys messing about on bikes, messing about in water, messing about in boats, and (according to his wife) messing about with mess. He's not a great sailor, but one day he'd like to join the crew of a replica Viking ship to follow the old Viking route from Scandinavia to the Shetland Islands and beyond. At some distant time in the future (maybe when he reaches 78 or so) he may grow up, but he's not promising anything.